BAT YAM

Bat Yam

H. C. Kim

The Hermit Kingdom Press
Cheltenham ♦ Seoul ♦ Bangalore ♦ Cebu

BAT YAM

Copyright © 2005 by H. C. Kim

Hardcover: ISBN 1-59689-016-9
Paperback: ISBN 1-59689-017-7
MS E-book: ISBN 1-59689-031-2

(USA) Library of Congress Control Number: 2005921627

Write-To Address:

The Hermit Kingdom Press
3741 Walnut Street, Suite 407
Philadelphia, PA 19104
United States of America

Info@TheHermitKingdomPress.com

* * * * *

Hermit Kingdom
12 South Bridge, Suite 370
Edinburgh, EH1 1DD
Scotland

http://www.TheHermitKingdomPress.com

For Adva and Shiry

Contents

"The sea appears all golden
Beneath the sun-lit sky."

Heinrich Heine

1
Bat Yam

It is nearly five o' clock, and I still see swimmers in the water, going this way and that. Some swim in a straight line, and others seem to be swimming in circles. Maybe that's what they want to do. From this angle, they all look like ants, anyway. I don't know why I enjoy looking down and seeing people swim below. Perhaps, it's a general fascination that people have looking at anything bustling. I remember, as a child I enjoyed watching whole families of ants gathering food and carrying it to their ant hills. And watching the bustle of a city and people moving about seemed fascinating for me. My curiosity would sometimes peak, and I would wonder what was the story behind all those people. I would try to garner information from people's facial expressions and hand gestures. Ah, that guy over there must be going to see his beloved!

But from this distance, I could neither see the food people below are carrying to their loved ones nor the facial expressions and the hand gestures. In fact, they seem like small dots moving this way and that. I am, after all, thirty floors above.

What am I doing here? I am visiting my friend Pierre, who recently made the decision to permanently move here. Pierre has been living in this country for over one year, but it is fairly recent that he made the decision to make a new life in this new land. This new apartment that Pierre moved into is a marker of the major transition in his life. The new building was opened to tenants just last week. This apartment has never been lived in before, and I could almost smell the fresh paint on the walls. Walls were painted blue, sky blue. The color seems to blend in nicely with the horizontal view from the window. Blue, blue skies with hardly any clouds. The floor was absolutely shining like the white pearl jewelry on gift shop windows of fancy stores in the newly erected department store just two blocks away. I hope Pierre all the luck trying to keep this beautiful white marble-like floor clean.

The living room area was quite pleasant. Blue walls complemented the white floor nicely. And the new leather sofa set seemed to belong appropriately in one corner. In the middle of the semi-rectangular sofa set was a coffee table. It had a transparent glass top with wooden support. Pierre said that he liked this because it reminded him of what post-modernism would look as a piece of furniture. On top of the see-through glass coffee table, is a chess board with nicely hand-carved wooden chess pieces directly from Kenya. It serves as a reminder to Pierre of his favorite vacation of all time.

There are more reminders of his childhood trip in the apartment. A large flat wooden statue of an African family adorn the walls directly above the elongated sofa piece facing the large window by which I am standing. And there are African cloth and beads artistically adorning the side of the wall, which the other piece of the two piece sofa set is facing. The cloth is very colorful with bright colors of red, blue, and yellow. The beads are white and cascading down brown strings, which are hardly noticeable except for the bottom where the brown strings are hand-tied in knots.

This beautiful bead and cloth combination is somewhat distracting when I wanted to watch the TV on the set directly below. I question Pierre's judgment in placing such a beautiful and eye catching combination art right above such a mundane piece of modern entertainment. But I will not mention this to him until later, much later. Right now, I am here to provide Pierre with encouragement and support.

I look over towards the sofa from the window area, and notice that the headset of the cordless phone is on the glass coffee table. I walk over in order to rejoin the phone to its base where battery can be charged. There is a large dining room table between me and the sofa area. I take couple steps and push in the dining room chair that occupies the head place on the table that stands parallel to the wide translucent window. As I walk past the dining room table and across the large open space between the dining room table and the coffee table, I notice to my right a book in the midst of a number of books that I haven't noticed before. I veer to my right and walk over to the book shelves by the wall. I reach over and pick out the book, *Let's Go Israel and Egypt*.

I am surprised that I have never seen this copy before. I thought I knew all the books that Pierre had in this new land. It didn't look like a new copy, either. I turn to the Index to look up the entry, "Bat Yam." I don't see it. So, I turn to the index for "Jerusalem" and find the pages containing information for that city. I skim over the pages. I am not so interested in seeing the information contained therein about the city and what kind of things one can do and enjoy. I am now more interested in seeing clues, any markings, that show how this book was used by Pierre. After all, Pierre and I had spent the whole of last year together in Jerusalem as roommates. How come I have never seen this copy of the seemingly used guide book of the city? I become more curious and check the back of the cover page to see if there's any name or anything else that might be written there. Nothing. I put the book back in the book shelf and turn left to head towards the coffee table.

While looking through the guidebook in search of clues, I had a feeling that the phone would ring. I wasn't doing anything wrong, but I felt like I was. I felt almost like reading a personal letter of someone without being granted permission. I know, the book was on the bookshelf for common perusal. There is an implicit understanding that permission is granted by the owner to visitors to look through his book collection in the living room. It's not like a personal letter that one doesn't want others to read, or some other secret that one wants to hide from the other. But for some reason, I felt that I was prying into an aspect of Pierre's life that I did not know or one that Pierre did not want to share with me. It's irrational, but that guilty feeling was there, and I quickly looked over the phone headset. I could probably just ask Pierre in passing about noticing the book, and I bet he would tell me. I didn't think we really had secrets between us. And what kind of secret could there be with a guide book?

Thoughts of guilt are lingering in my mind as I pick up the phone headset. Since the base of the cordless phone is behind the sofa facing the television, I walk around that sofa piece. I place the headset onto the phone base. I remember doing this numerous times in Jerusalem. Pierre had a habit of forgetting to put the phone headset on the base after talking on the phone. I told him casually and not seriously at first to put the headset back on the base. Please, I entreated him. When he did not seem to take my request seriously, I even sat him down to explain to him that if the phone headset doesn't get charged at the base and the battery is all gone, then the phone will not function. It was the only phone we had in our Jerusalem apartment. But either this concept did not register in his mind or he just simply forgot.

I knew that he wasn't doing it out of spite. Pierre was just too good natured and kindhearted to do that. Also, he had an aristocratic upbringing, and politeness was emphasized over all else. Even when one was upset, sad, happy, or mad, one needed to be polite. This was the appropriate thing to do. It would go against his whole life teaching to act out of spite, to be rude in not fulfilling the request. Maybe, one of the reasons why Pierre did not replace the headset on the phone base was that I was doing it for him when he did not. I did not want to test this theory out because what if the battery did not recharge and we were out of phone service for a while? We could miss an important phone call. We might need to make a needed phone call and we would have to walk all the way down the street to public phones to make a phone call. I often did not have a phone card with more than twenty units. What if I had to make a call to the US? I would have to go some five blocks to the store that sells phone cards. If it's the evening, I would have to wait until the morning. So, it was just easier to replace the phone headset, myself. In fact, it is this very headset and phone base that occupied a little time of my everyday life in Jerusalem.

Pierre liked this phone very much. He liked the mobility it provided. Once he even commented that he felt free like a bird with this cordless phone. He didn't feel constrained or confined, like when he used phones with headsets attached to the base by a cord. He told me that in France he even once got a long cord to give him extra mobility to make himself feel more free and tripped over the line and sprained his wrist. It took couple weeks for the wrist to heel. Since it was his writing hand, he wasn't able to write properly or profusely like he liked to do, for couple weeks. No such accidents were possible with the cordless phone. Since he expressed more than a few times how much he liked my cordless phone, I decided to give it to him as his housewarming gift. I am leaving to go back to America in a few days and lightening my load isn't such a bad idea, either. Besides, it always made me happy to see Pierre happy.

Pierre said that he would call if he was going to be late, but he hasn't, yet. So, it isn't just any telephone ring that made me conscious of what I was doing; it was the fact that Pierre could call any moment and I didn't want to be caught with my hands on the guide book. In fact, Pierre could walk through that door, any moment. But since he was late, I figured there was more chance of my receiving his phone call, than being surprised by his abrupt and tarried entrance. Of course, this was an irrational sense of guilt. I wasn't doing anything wrong by going through the guide book.

Since I am doing an errand of sorts by replacing the headset on the phone base, I decide to treat myself to something. The phone is on a table against the wall and directly diagonal to the phone to the right at about 45 degrees is the doorway to the kitchen. The passage way catches my eye. What better way to treat oneself than with something in the refrigerator? Life's simple pleasures, I tell myself. I walk over to the entrance way. It takes about four steps to get over there. I feel like I am in the times of pirates and hidden treasures. Didn't they count distances by steps, like I was doing in this apartment? I don't know why I am doing this, really. I don't normally count steps. I guess, partly, I am bored. And there is a small part of me that is holding onto the fascination that I felt when I heard from a premier Israeli archaeologist about how ancient Israelites measured distances in terms of the length from the tip of the middle finger to the pointed elbow end of a bent arm. This is the reason why the distances in the ancient times varied, since each person most likely had a different arm length. The whole concept of using one's body as a measuring tool is an interesting concept. We use the term "foot" and "feet." I bet these go back to measuring with the named term, namely one's foot. I have to look this up when I get back to the US, I make a mental note for myself.

As soon as I enter the doorway into the kitchen, I turn to my right for my prize. The refrigerator is right there waiting to be opened. I take hold of the brand new handle to the new large refrigerator and looked inside. There is a half-used butter and a jar of almost empty jam that I had placed in the refrigerator that morning after breakfast. I know Pierre doesn't normally keep jam in the refrigerator. He keeps his jam along with sugar, salt, and coffee in one of the cabins next to the refrigerator. I always put jam inside the refrigerator. Maybe, it was my blind obedience to the command in the label of jams that I use in the US: Refrigerate after opening! I wonder if that imperative is written on this jam jar. I take out the jam jar and look through the Hebrew words. I see a pronouncement, "Kosher for

Passover" in Hebrew, but I cannot see any demands for refrigeration. Is jam here made differently than in the US? It can't be just an Israeli thing since Pierre is from France and that is the normative practice there from what I could garner from him. I put the jam back with questions of cultural relativity and how that might apply to food. "You think too much." I remember my mom's words, and I smile.

With a smile on my face, I look through the refrigerator for my award. There it is, a bottle of Diet Coke. It is one of those 1.5 liter bottles. Two liter bottles are just so much more practical, I say to myself as I take the new bottle of Diet Coke out. The words, "Always Coca Cola" in Hebrew capture my eyes. Some things are consonant, I think to myself. Kind of like McDonald's. I remember when the first McDonald's opened its doors in my favorite city center in Jerusalem. Some of my American friends used to say after hearing the prophecy of its advent in the city that it's a shame that America's cultural imperialism was entering this country. I wanted to see how it would be, so I went to McDonald's quite soon after it opened. Would people like it? Were there going to be protesters in front of it demonstrating against American cultural imperialism? My questions were quickly answered in my first visit. I remember only happy, smiling faces ordering Big Mac's and no profane Hebrew words directed adversely against this fine American establishment. McDonald's even made efforts to cater to those in Jerusalem who kept kosher. The dietary laws of traditional Judaism demands that one does not mix meat with milk products like cheese. Big Mac certainly would be a violation of this dietary rule, so this branch of McDonald's offered Big Mac's without cheese. Now, even traditionally observant could consume the great American national symbol and participate in what is becoming a global culture. I figure that I saw exactly what I expected. McDonald's always survives and thrives – like America. There had been questions about whether McDonald's would do well in the culinary paradise of France. The question is now mute. The McDonald's along the Champs Elysee is always packed. This is a claim not too many neighboring restaurants could make. And I remember being in Moscow at the biggest McDonald's that I have been to in my life and it was packed there as well. McDonald's seems to enjoy the same kind of popularity everywhere I've been to. So it's no surprise that it was so popular in Jerusalem.

But the idea of McDonald's as an American cultural imperialist tool is an interesting one. Pierre had repeatedly commented to me that Americans have no culture. I told him that we have a beautiful culture and history. He asked me to point out American culture. After futilely mentioning America's great literary figures and some of our cultural traditions like the Thanksgiving, I forwarded McDonald's as an American cultural symbol. It definitely is a common cultural symbol, I argued, since there probably isn't a child or adult in America who does not know McDonald's or Big Mac. It is a common bond and comprises a shared experience. Isn't that part of what culture is? Pierre told me that I was wrong and just dismissed my idea. I don't think it's wrong to say that McDonald's represents American culture to an extent. Why else would every other American go to McDonald's when they feel homesick or want something American?

Coca Cola is similar. I have heard the phrase, as American as Apple Pie. Well, that phrase doesn't quite make sense outside of the US. As American as McDonald's or Coca Cola would probably make more sense, abroad. I was proud to be holding a piece of American culture in my hands. During my travels, I've heard people say that you become more patriotic when you travel abroad. I think there is certainly an element of truth in this. It might be that in the sea of differences and unfamiliarity, one harkens back to the place that gives one's distinctiveness a collective identity. In America, there is a shared culture and the fact that one is an American is a non-issue. One doesn't consciously have to think about it. But abroad, when one sees everyone doing things differently from himself and that is the norm, he longs to feel normal and, therefore, harkens back to the calm sea of familiarity that one left behind for an overseas adventure. That could be one explanation. Or, it might simply be national pride in the way one feels proud when an American athlete wins a gold metal in the Olympics. I am proud that Coca Cola has done so well abroad. I pour this cultural trophy into a tall glass cup and begin to partake of my prize. I remember how much I like the taste of Diet Coke, although I could almost swear it seems to taste a little different than Diet Coke I've consumed in constant flow back in the US.

I remember a discussion with some Americans traveling in Venice over some authentic Italian pizza in the heart of the ethereal city about the nature of Coke. John was convinced that the water in local lands affect the way that Coke tastes, and he swore that there were differences in taste. I never really thought about different taste of Coke across lands before that conversation in any critical way. What started out as simple dinner conversation ended up in my consciousness when drinking Coca Cola products in my travels. Maybe, what John said is affecting my judgment. Maybe, I am looking for differences where there were none. I remember talking with Kate about the distinction between Coke and Pepsi. She said there was none. In order to prove this, she exchanged her best friend's Coke with Pepsi without telling her about the change. Kate mentioned that her best friend lived in the Coke City and swore by the product, so she was most apt for the test. When Kate asked her best friend whether she noticed any difference in taste, she answered and even swore that there was none. And there it was. Kate had changed her best friend's Coke with Pepsi and she did not notice the difference. Could it be that sometimes we imagine differences where there are none?

After taking a couple sips of my Diet Coke, I grab a chair couple steps away from the refrigerator. It's the kitchen table that Pierre and I used for our breakfast of toast with jam and coffee in one of those really big coffee cups that looked more like a big soup bowl than a coffee cup. Our tradition in Jerusalem was to boil half a cup of milk and mix it up with a half a cup of filtered coffee in a big coffee bowl. Some traditions are not so bad to maintain.

I notice a small drop of coffee on the white table that somehow was missed by my sponge bath of the table. I put my glass of Diet

Coke down right on top of the small coffee stain. I will probably spill some Diet Coke, so I'll take care of all the stains together afterwards. Efficiency. I sit on a chair without back support and realize how uncomfortable that is. In the morning, I guess I didn't think about that being hungry and just out of my dream voyage. And I did have a nice dream last night.

I dreamt that I was flying high over the skies. It was so blue and so clear without even one speck of cloudmass. I felt the warmth of the sun on my body as I flew through the skies. I felt free like a bird. There were no restraints or obstacles along the way. I bet, driving on the autobahn in a clear day without any traffic may give a taste of this dream in real life. I understand that some parts of Montana don't have speed limits any more, either. "Live Free or Die!" I remember reading in a New Hampshire license plate. The feeling of freedom is a great thing. How wonderful that freedom is an ideal in the US! A very worthy virtue.

I sip my ice cold Diet Coke, just the way I like it. And I look up from the small Kitchen table, which leans against the wall. At about the eye level is an overblown picture of a banana split. I guess it's not an inappropriate picture to adorn the kitchen wall. The picture must be a hundred times the real size. I see the three scoops of ice cream – strawberry, chocolate, and vanilla – sandwiched between two slices of banana with lots of whipped cream on top and a very bright and inviting cherry on the top. I can see the strawberry and chocolate syrup. That would be more like a prize, I think to myself. I haven't had a banana split since I got to Israel about a year ago. I'm sure I could find it somewhere, but it was never my priority to look. Ice cream bars and cones served their purpose well enough during hot summer days. And I never had a sweet tooth. But it feels like somehow the sweet tooth ferry has gotten hold of me, now, possessed me. I long for that banana split on the wall. That exact, same one. I guess, advertisements do really work. Of course, this is supposed to be a piece of art. The picture is nicely framed and may even have some monetary value. Now, however, it feels like a big and effective advertisement for banana splits. How I want that banana split! I quickly drink my Diet Coke, less satisfied with it than when I first took out with pride the bottle of Diet Coke from the refrigerator.

I bring my empty glass and rinse it out on the sink. I notice that I haven't put the Diet Coke bottle back in the refrigerator, yet. Turning my back to the banana split on the wall, I gently place the Diet Coke bottle back into the refrigerator. This time, my palates peaked by the visual stimulant, I notice how empty the refrigerator is and feel a bit of pain in my stomach. Basically, there is nothing more than the half-consumed butter and the almost empty jam jar. There are some vegetables, but they don't look too fresh, either. No wonder that Pierre said he needed to go grocery shopping along with other errands. I should have pressed to go with him, but it sounded like he had some personal errands to do.

I walk towards the other end of the kitchen. There's also a window looking out into the beautiful Mediterranean shoreline. It's a good seven steps away from the refrigerator. I stand beside the window and look out. It's the same familiar bright blue sky that welcomes me. And below, I see the little dots moving this way and that. I reach over and pull the lever of the window and open it wide. I can smell the salt water and even feel like the salt in the air is settling in my skin. I hear voices of dots below. They are joyful sounds. I hear these sounds of entertainment mixed with those of frolicking seagulls. The water is full of people, still; the sun doesn't want to leave this beach paradise even though the evening is edging closer.

I put my hand out the window and feel the warm air. I feel like I could grab the humidity in the air. Warmth turns from being pleasant to being oppressive. Beads of sweat start forming, and I feel myself perspiring already. I had just opened the window, few minutes ago. I close the window quickly and take couple steps back to feel the coolness of the apartment. I can feel the cool air enwrapping me and clothing me with coolness. I exit through the other kitchen door right next to the kitchen window that leads into the dining area. Now, I have made an elliptical loop around the apartment, and I am back in my original spot by the dining area window. I take my former posture by the window. I lean my right hand and elbow against the window pane and draw my face very close to the window as if I were drawing close to kiss the love of my life. I look out the window. But this time I want to take a seat. So, I take couple steps away from the window to pull out the dining room chair at the head of the dinner table. I bring the chair closer to the window. I position the chair so that it is not facing directly toward the outside world. Rather, I place it parallel to the window. If I were to sit straight, I would be facing a wall. But even while sitting, I hold on to my previous form. I sit, turn my body towards the window with my hand and elbow against the window pane. My left leg is outstretched and my right leg is slightly bent, facing towards the window. My right knee is slightly touching the bottom part of the wide window. I draw my face closer and closer to the window, this time more slowly than the last.   And I look into the endless blue skies.

2

Operation Food Know

It seems like yesterday when I first met Pierre. I remember walking through the apartment door and seeing him for the first time. He looked visibly French wthdark hair and tanned skin. His English sounded quite unrehearsed and unused. I managed to understand what he was saying. After confirming that he was from France, I tried out my French. I had two years of college level French and felt pretty confident. Despite my self-assured demeanor, my French to Pierre's ears must have been like his English to my ears. Pierre was patient and told me that my French was nice. In the midst of two spoken languages, Pierre and I managed to strike a conversation and a bond.

But it really wasn't the fact that we were able to speak to each other that a bond of sorts was formed. I liked Pierre the moment he opened the door. There was gentleness in his gaze and a slight abashedness in his demeanor. Yet, Pierre was polite and seemed polished in his manners. He offered me something to drink as soon as introductions were done. I considered declining, but it was a warm summer day and I had lugged two big pieces of luggage up a hill and then a short but seemingly endless staircase.

Although it was the first time we ever saw each other, I knew that we would become good friends. It was a combination of my first impression of him and intuition. And sure enough, within less than a week after we became roommates, we became good friends, pouring our souls to each other. Soon after that, we started to devise a program. I refer to the plan that Pierre and I concocted as a type of a social program in the sense that we were exploring ways to get to know more people in the area. As it is always easier to do such things as a team effort, we needed each other to work together to make this social program a reality. And what was this social program?

We scheduled to get to know new people roughly in our age group, preferably of female gender, by inviting them home for a wonderful meal and conversation. We dubbed the project, Operation Food Know. This seemed like the most efficient way to get to know people well. And since Pierre came from France and I came from the USA, we did not have any good friends in Jerusalem. Operation Food Know seemed like a solution to solve that problem. I took upon myself the role of inviting people to dinner and being the social director, and Pierre took upon himself the role of a cook. We would work together to clean up afterwards. So, the stage was set for the newly formed friendship to function as a purposeful coalition for getting to know people -- more specifically, Israeli women. Neither of us had as our specific purpose getting to know women exclusively for romantic reasons, however.

Both of us were united in our under-standing that things just happen. We would get to know some nice young ladies and if the fortunes shine favorably upon us, there might be mutual sparks and romance might develop. But we were pleased to get to know nice people and considered friendships that could develop from Operation Food Know as almost an equal blessing.

I was excited at the newly formed pact for the common good – well, as it pertained to us. But realization set in shortly afterwards that all the initial responsibility was up to me. I was the one who had to find the young ladies to invite to the creative and enjoyable dinner that Pierre and I have talked *ad nauseam* into imaginary reality. We were so enthusiastic, and in the midst of the excited conversation, I had dismissed the logistical difficulties in-volved in such a venture. When the calm settled, I realized that it was difficult enough to get a completely unfamiliar person to get together even for a cup of coffee, let alone have that person come to dinner at your place. Doesn't that take at least several prolonged communications in different settings?

Furthermore, not only was I to invite one person, I had to ask her to bring her friend to join me and my roommate Pierre, whom she hasn't met yet. How was she going to explain things to her friend whom she wanted to bring along, supposing that I get that far? Ummm, there is this American guy who invited me to dinner at his place and he wanted me to bring along a friend because he's throwing the dinner along with his roommate. The name of the roommate? Ummm, it is some French sounding name, but I forgot. How many women would agree to come for dinner under these circumstance? Dinner at home is not like dinner in a restaurant, either. In a restaurant, at least there is a sense that it is a neutral territory. With dinner at home, it's the turf of the host. One can't knock the value of home court advantage, or the visiting team's disadvantage.

Especially in light of the fact that Pierre and I were completely new to the area, there wouldn't be too many places to seek our references, as it would be possible, say with other Israeli students. Someone was bound to know something about an Israeli guy that's extending the invitation to dinner. But a couple of foreign guys? Furthermore, who knows what these American and French guys are capable of? Most likely, the women who are invited would be Israelis and probably did not have too many encounters with Americans or the French. The fear of the unknown is always there. Isn't that a natural human instinct and the pitfall of potential tolerance in different societies? There is nothing more fearful than the unknown. I realized that logistically this was going to be very difficult.

Of course, I am no defeatist and I wasn't going to let a small obstacle get in the way of our mutual American-French pact. Not only did we have our individual pride at stake here, but much more was at stake here. Our ability to bond with Israelis would prove the feasibility of such a bond for anyone else who would try. We are being trailblazers. With this renewed sense of mission to invigorate myself and be imbued with courage, I set out for the city.

I walked up to the bus stop and waited for the Egged public bus. There was a bench, so I took my seat. Next to me was an Israeli soldier sitting there with a M16 machine gun. I had never seen a M16 up that close before, so I couldn't help but stare at the gun. Then, I heard a voice asking me something in Hebrew. I looked up and there was a very beautiful young Israeli woman, who could not have been more than in her early twenties. She had long dark hair that almost came to her shoulders. Her eyes were brown and some-what piercing at me. They stood in contrast to her smooth olive colored skin and gently flowing lips. For a second, I was amazed at her beauty, and, the next second, I was amazed at myself for not having noticed such a beautiful face, right away. I guess the fact that she was wearing an army uniform and had a machine gun right by her side in a very prominent place was distracting enough. And she did have her head turned slightly side ways and away from me, perhaps looking at something down the street, when I came up and sat down.   I immediately started to stare at her M16, and her response was almost immediate.   She looked at me, and words darted out of her mouth almost defensively.

My modern Hebrew conversation skill was not really existent at the moment, so I replied back in English. I told her that I didn't quite understand her as I was currently attending an intensive modern Hebrew conversation course.   For some reason she started to smile. Maybe, it was the fact that she managed to intimidate someone much bigger than her in size. She had a M16, for God's sake!   Or, perhaps she thought my learning modern Hebrew conversation was something that was neat. What I wanted to believe was that she was captivated by my looks, and the sound of my voice melted her heart in an instant, filling her with the realization that she was experiencing love at first sight.

She looked absolutely ravishing as the blaring fire in her eyes turned into a warm hearth of a family fire place. She looked at me for a second and asked me if I was new to her country. I told her that I have been there for only a few weeks. I was trying to get my bearing of the place. I told her of my eagerness to learn more about her country. This comment seemed to go over well with her, and she asked me immediately if I liked her country. I told her that, so far, I was fascinated by her country. I couldn't help but confess to her that she was the first female soldier with a machine gun that I saw in my life. She looked pleasantly surprised, the way Annie looked when I told her that she had a mean side. Annie is the sweetest person in the world, almost a living angel. One time I thought that she did something not so kind, so I told her that she had a mean side. Instead of getting angry, she smiled and looked like she just received a complement. I was puzzled at the moment, because who likes to hear that they are mean? The young Israeli soldier had what I thought to be the same expression then. Maybe, it made her feel powerful? A young beautiful woman with soft features in a generic army uniform with a fighting war weapon.

I wasn't sure what to make of her and her facial response, so I commented that I thought that she was the most beautiful soldier that I have ever seen in my life. I wasn't sure if this complement was appropriate or not according to Israeli standards, but I have always been an honest, upfront kind of a person, so I was just telling her what I was thinking. Of course, being a little bit nervous might have made me more direct than I was accustomed to. She smiled. And she let out a cute giggle. I asked her what her name was. It's Orit. I told her that it was a beautiful name. Does it have any meaning? Orit told me that it means Little Light, since *or* is Hebrew for Light and *it* is a diminutive. She sure shone like a beautiful light in that street. She asked me what my name was. I told her that it was Samuel. She asked me if I were Jewish. I was somewhat taken aback by this question. It was the first time that I was asked this question. Also, living in America, I was not accustomed to someone asking me about my religious affiliation right away. I successfully caught my expression of utter surprise before it became evident to her and managed to say that I am not. I told her that I am a Christian. She asked, then, what I was doing in her country. I told her that I was here to learn modern Hebrew and to work as a volunteer in a nearby archaeological dig.

Just in that moment, the bus pulled up to the bus stand. We both looked at each other and stood up. I waited for Orit to step in front of me. She gave me a smile as she stepped up onto the bus steps. I couldn't help but notice her shapely figure from the behind. As she bent her leg to step up into the bus, I noticed the curves of her calves and the firmness of her thighs accentuating the lines on her pants. The curve lines followed all the way to her buttocks. I remember my best friend telling me once in the US about a butt you could bounce a quarter off of. Orit had such a characteristic about her. I didn't want to seem like I was staring, so I quickly stepped up the bus stairs as well. I was just inches behind Orit, and I could smell her hair. It smelled like fresh spring flowers that I smelled while walking along Longwood Gardens in Pennsylvania.

As she turned slightly towards the driver and dropped her coins into the machine, I could see that she had a nice long neck and that the side view of her face was just as beautiful as her front facial view. After she paid for her fair, she walked along the isle. I had forgotten to get my coins out. I was preoccupied with Orit's flowery odor and was in the middle of a short visual voyage. I got my wallet out and paid with a bill. I grabbed the first bill. It would have taken too much time to take out my coins and count them. I didn't want to irritate the driver by doing that. But it seemed that my good intentions did not go appreciated. The driver looked at me, said something in Hebrew which did not sound like a friendly invitation to dinner, and handed me back my change. He had a reason to be upset. I gave him the biggest common bill in Israeli currency. I received several paper bills and some coins in return. I told him, thank you, in modern Hebrew and then looked towards the isle.

I was hoping that Orit had sat with an empty seat next to her. And sure enough, she did. But this didn't mean much since the bus was practically empty. If the bus were full, and she chose a seat with an empty seat next to her, then there is a possibility that she did that so that I could come and join her. In the same situation, she could choose to sit in a seat without any open seats and that could be a sign that she was no longer interested to chat with me. But as the bus was practically empty, I didn't know how to read this. Also, because of my delay in paying for the bus fare and getting back my change, she had already gone down midway down the isle and sat down. Had I had correct change readily available, I could have just walked right behind her and sat down next to her in a natural way. Now, it was going to be more unnatural, walking down the bus isle and sitting down next to her, or even near her, for that matter. Bus was practically empty, so it could look a little odd. But I really wanted to talk a little more with her in the least. I walked down the isle.

When I was halfway from where she was sitting, the bus made a sharp turn. I don't think the bus driver used breaks as he made that turn. I almost fell down the isle but quickly caught hold of a seat next to me. My natural instinct was to sit down on either of the empty seats to the right or left of me. But I knew that it would mean the end of my conversation with Orit and, maybe, no chance of ever seeing her again. I looked up after I caught myself and caught the concern in Orit's eyes. Encouraged by this, I continued to walk down the isle, and Orit asked me if I were all right. By the time she ended up asking me this question, I was standing right near her. I said, I'm fine, thank you. And she moved her M16 towards the window of the bus, so I took the cue and sat down next to her.

Two-person seats in the bus did not leave much space between the two sitting individuals. I immediately found my arm touching her arm. Her army shirt sleeves have been neatly rolled up above her elbows. I don't know if it was because she was warm in that uniform or if it was a fashion statement she was making. A kind of rebellion for her feminine beauty against the generic uniform she was wearing. Whatever her intentions, it sure had the effect of accentuating her beautiful characteristics. Her arms were golden olive and smooth. I felt the smooth texture of her arm in my own arm. My left arm had been touching her right arm for nearly five seconds, and she has not yet pulled her arm away. I realized that my left leg was slightly touching her right leg, as well. There wasn't that much room for the passengers, I thought. But I felt like hugging every Egged bus designer in sight at that moment.

Orit then tossed me a question. What do you think about Israeli women? I wonder if she noticed my face turning bright red. I was hoping that my face has turned tan enough in the Mediterranean sun environment for her not to notice the color change in my face. I looked at her and with the utmost composure I could gather, I told her that I didn't know enough Israeli women to do justice to her question. But I added that I thought that Israeli women that I have seen were beautiful. She smiled and said, really? She almost seemed like she didn't believe me. I smiled back at her an affirmation of my previous statement.

I thought to myself how nice it would be actually to get to know this person better and simultaneously words accompanied my thoughts out of my lips. Orit seemed not unhappy with my sharing of this sentiment with her. I thought that the best thing was to be totally honest with her. So, I began to describe to her Operation Food Know for to getting to know Israelis by inviting them for dinner at our place. I did leave out the detail that these dinner invitations would be extended only to Israeli women. I think I was wise to leave that little part out. Orit replied that she would love to participate in this program. I was taken a little aback by her enthusiasm. Mom was right: Honesty is the best policy. I asked her if she had any roommates whom she could bring with her. Orit did have a roommate. And her name was Orli. Orit told me that the name means, Light For Me. *Or* means Light and *li* means For Me. I wondered if this Light For Me was just as beautiful as Little Light. Lights seemed to be forming a bright constellation in my little corner of the universe.

Orit broke my mental journey into the outer reaches of universal paradiso with the question, Can I bring something. I responded by saying that she did not need to bring anything, except for her wonderful smile. I told her that Pierre is French and hinted at the culinary possibilities that awaited her and her roommate. After all, wasn't France the land of Food, Wine, and Cheese? Everyone knows that the best chefs are in France. How could some of that glorious food culture not have rubbed off on Pierre? It seemed clear to me that mentioning that he is French was sufficient enough to indicate that the dinner promised to be a supreme adventure of sorts.

But then, I remembered Pierre using ketchup as his spaghetti sauce. He assured me that it was the French way for one to cook up pasta and use ketchup as tomato sauce. As any red-blooded American could well imagine, I was horrified at this. One puts ketchup on hamburgers and hotdogs and french fries. But certainly not on spaghetti. They sold bottles and cans of tomato sauce in numerous variety for the purpose of applying on and consuming with spaghetti. I had waited for Pierre to tell me that it was a big joke and that he was pulling my American leg. But that awakening never came. And more frequently I saw him consuming spaghetti with ketchup. Then it happened. I saw him and another French friend consuming spaghetti with ketchup, together. That confirmed it. That was not an unacceptable practice in France. And, gasp, it might even be seen as normative. When I remembered these episodes, I felt compelled to forward a stronger recommendation of Pierre's culinary experiences. Who knows, perhaps Orit had seen some French people eating spaghetti with ketchup as well. I told her that Pierre has recipes from his mom back in France and they are incredible. And this was the honest-to-God truth. Although Pierre did make spaghetti with ketchup in his busier moments, when he took the time to make a normal meal, it was quite amazing. I just had to make sure that Pierre had ample time to cook in the evening when the two Lights descend upon our humble abode. No spaghetti with ketchup on that night!

After elaborating as much as I could on Pierre's culinary expertise and when I almost felt her salivation beneath her closed lips, I asked her the question, did she ever see someone eat spaghetti with ketchup? She literally gasped. Spaghetti with ketchup? I felt like I was accused of a crazy act, so I quickly added that I had seen someone do that and I was just as shocked. Absolutely shocked. I had never tried it even once and was afraid to find out how it tasted. This seemed to put her mind to rest. I was a normal person in her view. I know that eating spaghetti with ketchup is no great sin. It might even taste good. Who knows? But I also knew that women don't like weird guys. At that moment, my bravery to argue for culinary diversity and the merits of that was overtaken by my more baser desire to see her in my apartment with her Light complement. I was, after all, at the prime of my manhood and my hormones were working effectively. Besides, I didn't feel that I was violating my ethical imperatives, since I could always bring up the important topic of cultural acceptance and tolerance of differences over the dinner when the harmony and good will fill the brightly lit dining room in the apartment of two very happy young men.

I knew that my stop was coming up soon, so I asked her for her phone number. She swiftly provided the valuable information on a piece of paper with the pen that I had ready. When I got her phone number, I told her that my bus stop was coming up soon. And I told her that I was very happy to meet her, that day. She said she was happy as well. I replied that I looked forward to seeing her soon. I stood up and went out through the nearby side door of the bus. As I exited the doorway, I quickly turned around to see her face once more. I was a bit embarrassed to see her staring in my direction. I gave her a smile and a short cute wave good-bye. I saw the bus go off after the doors closed behind me.

3

Mahaneh Yehudah

That night, I broke the good news to Pierre. Pierre was thrilled. A beautiful Israeli soldier. Wow, he said. We began to strategize. What were we going to make? This was going to be our first Operation Food Know dinner for Israeli Women. It was special, and we wanted to accord all honor due to this event. We decided that the dessert should be nothing short of heavenly. What came closest to being heavenly? Chocolate mousse, of course. Mai, oui! Pierre had never made chocolate mousse before. That required a quick phone call back to the Land of Fine Cuisine. But before he made that phone call to his mom, we had to decide what we were going to make for an appetizer and for the main entree.

Pierre suggested making some kind of pasta for the main course. Flashbacks to spaghetti with ketchup were ubiquitous as soon as the suggestion for pasta was put on the table. What if something went wrong and we were out of time? I didn't want Pierre even to be tempted to use ketchup as spaghetti sauce. Another of mom's advice: Always hope for the best but expect the worst. I quickly steered Pierre away from any Pasta dishes; I was just applying life philosophy that I was raised on. We decided on honey glazed chicken. Pierre was going to ask his mom for the recipe to this dish, too. Although I was no cook -- both Pierre and I knew this so patently well -- I wanted to partake of the preparations for this momentous feast that could mark a turning point in our lives. It certainly had all the makings of a high point of our stay in this new land. I remembered really liking the fried vegetables that mom cooked up. Maybe, I could make that. It didn't seem like they involved complex combinations of sauces where things could go really wrong. I decided to call mom back in the States. So it was set. We had an appetizer, main course, and dessert. Now, we had to go shopping for all the ingredients.

There was only one place to go to do the shopping for this momentous occasion. We didn't have to ask each other where we were going to acquire raw materials for Operation Food Know. There was an inaudible but clear call from Mahaneh Yehudah, the open market of fresh vegetables and produce near the heart of the city. I went to bed that night looking forward to this preparatory stage to the monumental feast. As I lay there on the bed of the apartment that was to be the setting of premier entertainment for two lovely ladies in a short while, I thought of how beautiful Orit looked. Her smile stamped a lasting imprint in my memory. I felt I could smell her hair, even now. I thought about what she will wear and how she will look in civilian clothing. It was going to be so nice getting to know her and connecting with her as I did, today.

I don't know when I drifted asleep, but the next thing I remember was dreaming. Surprisingly, I didn't dream about Orit. That would have been the natural process since I fell asleep thinking about her and even getting a little excited at the prospect of seeing her again. My body was definitely anticipating this glorious event. Yet, it was not about Orit, but about the Jerusalem market place that I dreamed. The image was clear in my mind as if I were there. I was walking down the narrow streets of Jerusalem on the way to Mahaneh Yehudah. I could see that there were others who were hurrying towards the hallowed sanctuary of fresh and healthy food. I had my empty backpack. After all, that was the most convenient way to transport the plethora of purchased items back. And often, my eyes were bigger than my stomach, as the Israelis would say in modern Hebrew.

Okay, maybe, this is not the appropriate application of that saying, since it referred to the consumption of food rather than shopping for food. But the saying can easily extend to include shopping. For instance, one eats because one sees how tasty the food is. And by the time one stops eating, it's possible that the consumption has passed the limited capacity. In the same way, when one looks at all the tasty fruits and vegetables, it's possible to purchase way more than one needs. The principle is the same. Haven't you ever heard of the saying that you should shop on a full stomach? That was also one of mom's sayings. It makes sense, since if one is hungry, one can easily fall into the mistaken perception that one has an unlimited capacity to consume. And more things look tasty when one is hungry than when one is not hungry. It's kind of like walking in the desert for days without water and then seeing a mirage of water in the distance. Eyes can play tricks on you. Okay, admittedly, in regards to the desert mirage imagery, I speak only from a theoretical perspective from watching the Bugs Bunny cartoons that depict this possibility, but I have heard from other reliable sources that this does happen. I was a good boy of Jerusalem (the term applied to goody-two-shoes) and always carried a water bottle with me wherever I went in this semi desert area. But the sun was definitely a desert sun. So, it's theoretically possible that I might have experienced the Bugs Bunny in Dessert syndrome, had I not been prepared.

Thirst and hunger certainly must have an effect on the individual. Why else is there a saying that the way to man's heart is through his stomach? Okay, this might not be a saying most in keeping with the times, but one cannot deny the fact that it is a common saying and existent in our cultural dictionary. Everybody knows about it. Implicit in this statement is the idea that a man could actually fall in love with a woman because of the way she cooks. Food and the corresponding satiation of hunger in a satisfactory manner can influence perception. I know plenty of guys who have applied this philosophy in the opposite direction. The way to a woman's heart is through her stomach. After all, wasn't Pierre's and my efforts in this vein? We were trying to cook up a storm in order to win the hearts, or at least gain friendships, of two Israeli women. Of course, we can say that we were just creating a context in which we wanted to get to know them better. But that would not be totally accurate. There was certainly a causative element related to food that played a role in the whole equation. Why did we pick this context over any other?

Going back to the dream, there I was walking towards Mahaneh Yehudah with my empty backpack. Pierre was at my side like Bat Man and Robin Hood in crusading search for fresh produce. I heard the familiar shouts of the Jerusalem open market as I drew closer to the bustling crowd. Tomatoes for two shekels! One pound of tomatoes for two shekels! Melodiously these modern Hebrew words rang out. I heard yet another voice not so far away from there. Mangos for ten shekels! One pound of mangos for ten shekels! Mangos are really good in Israel and very fresh. It was in season as well, which explains why they were so cheap. In the dream, I felt myself smiling and heading straight for the mangos. I bought a whole pound for ten shekels and I felt my back pack fill up as I placed what was sure to be juicy mangos inside.

The next scene in the dream, as I remember it, was not a picture of me carrying the load of mangos back to my apartment nor of further shopping for fresh fruits and vegetables. Rather, I was instantaneously placed in my dining room area cutting the mangos into nice square patterns in a way that an older Israeli gentleman had shown me once in the market place. The method was a new discovery for me in Israel. The artistry of mango consumption started out very much like what I was used to in America. We cut mangos by each side with the effect that in the end almost a square surrounding the mango seed is left with four large pieces of mango meat with their outer skin left to consume. The difference is that in the US, I normally try to peel off the skin and consume the fleshy part. It is a little messy.

The method taught to me by an Israeli man sagacious in the art of mango consumption deviates from my formerly held method in that instead of peeling off the skin, the gentleman approached the flat surface of the fleshy part of the mango piece and cut lines diagonally and horizontally. After a grid pattern was made resembling the streets of New York City, the knife was taken away from the mango piece. The gentleman placed his thumbs on the side edges of the mango piece with the fleshy part facing towards his face and the rounded skin part away from him. He placed both his pointing fingers and index fingers on the skin part of the mango piece right near the center. Then, the gentleman pressed his index and pointing fingers towards his face and his thumbs away from him. I did exactly as he did. The effect was marvelous. The cut grid lines over the flat surface of the juicy mango piece came alive like what seemed like skyscrapers of New York City rising quickly towards me. And the mango chunk was ready to be consumed piece by piece as small blocks of mango begged patient consumption.

Whoever said that one cannot taste anything in a dream has not had a great dream. I tasted every piece of the juicy mango in my dream. I remember consuming one mango, then two, and then three, and basically making a meal out of it. I felt mango juice running down my hands and even down the my lower lips onto my chin. I smelled mango juice and the flagrance was almost intoxicating. I remember thinking in the dream that this must be so close to what heaven is like. I don't remember much after that. I must have woken up shortly afterwards. It was a new day and I was ready for Mahaneh Yehudah. I remember saying to myself then that I will certainly remember to pick up a mango or two or three, at least.

Pierre and I set out on our route to Mahaneh Yehudah. It was almost a weekly ritual to go shopping there. At first, it started out more or less for financial reasons. It was the place one could purchase produce for the cheapest price. Sometimes, the price of produce at the open market was as low as half the cost at a neighborhood grocery store. And the savings surely add up. What started out as a financial practicality ended up being a culinary necessity, however. Once we tasted the fresh vegetables and fruits at the Jerusalem market, purchases made at local grocery stores tasted somehow inferior. We began to feel that picking up goods for consumption at the neighborhood store was a form of culinary compromise. Although I would not elevate this to any form of ethical compromise, Pierre being French, perhaps, always seemed to have a guilty face whenever we went shopping at the neighborhood store to pick up some things that ran out during the week. Often, it wasn't worth the trip to pick up one of two things at the Jerusalem market, so compromises were made. But these occasions almost threw Pierre into a bad mood. Mahane Yehudah shopping seemed to have become an important part of Pierre's experience in Jerusalem, and, furthermore, it seemed to reassure him of his role as the guardian of all things culinary. Only a few times did I see sparks light up Pierre's eyes. And certainly talking about how good French cuisine was one of them. I knew that his excitement and pride in French cuisine would surely exhibit themselves in the dinner conversation that was to come. I knew this to be true as the earth is round and one plus one is two.

For me, it wasn't the culinary value of Jerusalem market food that was the driving force in this weekly ritual. I thought of Mahane Yehudah shopping as a form of entertainment. Let me clarify what I mean. I liked going to the market and seeing the bustle of people eagerly shopping for what would bring them happiness that night and for several days to come. People always seem to be in a better mood whenever they are shopping for food, for some reason. Food as a universal necessity often complements the unversality of the enjoyment of food. It's true that people from different cultures might like different kinds of food. Some people living in Asia might love spicy food. And some living in northern Europe might not be familiar with spicy food and find their enjoyment in foods that some of their Asian counterparts might find a little bland. But for people of all groups, good food is something to be celebrated. In both Asian and northern European cultures, as is the case in other cultures, people will go and pay a part of their hard earned money for the opportunity to consume fine food at a nice restaurant. Food seems to be a common denominator. It is no different at Mahane Yehudah. People look happier shopping for fresh produce and perhaps thinking about good food they would consume in the near future. Because food is a common denominator of sorts, people shopping at the market place become implicit partners. We are all shopping for food. There's nothing evil in food. In the same way that children like Barney because this purple monster embodies all things good and in their affection of this furry artificial being they are united, purchasing of food at Mahaneh Yehudah functions as a unifying factor. Buying food and eating represent a neutral or objective good in which consumers partake. The act of shopping for food at this market place and enjoying the process, which of course are inextricably linked to future consumption there of, are akin to the act of bonding that goes on with each child vis-à-vis the Purple Monster. Just as watching Barney is a form of entertainment as well as bonding, shopping at Mahaneh Yehudah has an element of bonding (to the market and to each other, the shoppers) as well as providing a form of entertainment. And at least subconsciously all in the market place partake in this entertainment.

Of course, the focus of entertainment might differ with individual persons. Different people might like an aspect of the shopping experience more than others. For instance, some might like to hear the call of the shopkeepers. Melodious sounds describing products linked to their prices often ring throughout the market and provide almost a liturgical experience. Some might like the part where some shopkeepers have free samples of their fresh produce handy for the customers. I was first introduced to real lychee fruit this way. I had consumed lychee fruit many times before in desserts, but often prepared. I did not know anything about how they were prepared and in what form they were plucked from the earth. In Mahane Yehudah, one day, I was given what was called a lychee fruit. I peeled off the thin hard shell and tasted the glorious, juicy, visibly more familiar fruit inside. Even without ice cream on the side, it tasted sweeter than my favorite mint chocolate chip ice cream. What began as one sample of lychee fruit ended up in my purchase of a whole batch of them. Purchase is recommended, but not obligatory for free samples. The most common samples are olives. Believe you me, they taste glorious. Nothing like the canned olives that we often find in our grocery stores in the US. Trying out free samples is fun and often a pleasing experience. And who doesn't like free stuff?

Others might like the experience of people watching in the market place. Some beautiful woman never fails to appear in Mahaneh Yehudah. For some, this might be a place to meet people. Who knows? I've never really met anyone in a market place that led to friendship or relationship, but my experience is not necessarily indicative of general trends. For instance, how many people could say that they met someone at the bus stop and were ready to invite her and her roommate to dinner? That experience, although it happened to me, is not usual or a common experience. I could surely not tell everyone that this is the way to meet people in Israel. It was my experience that others might share, but so far, not too many people that I talked to had similar experiences or results.

One thing is clear. Since there were beautiful women who almost never failed to show up at each of our outings to Mahane

Yehudah and, as you know, it was a weekly ritual, it would not have surprised me in the least bit if this experience was fairly common for other men as well. To say that this opportunity for appreciation was confined only to the male sex would most likely be a bad conclusion. There were often equal number of men and women shopping in the Jerusalem open market, so I am sure that there must have been more than a few women who enjoyed looking at good looking guys while partaking of their shopping experience. Pierre and I sure liked to think that we weren't in the bad looking category. Actually, I would have to say, I know that Pierre is probably in the exceptionally good looking category. There are several reasons that I think this.

First of all, many of my female friends in Israel throughout our one year of being roommates told me that Pierre was good looking. I was once told that women have hard time trusting Pierre because he was too good looking. Since more than one woman friend told me this, I had no reason to doubt their judgment. Another reason why I feel that women consider Pierre good looking is that everywhere we go, particularly when we went dancing in a night club, women never failed to congregate to where we are dancing. And often I have caught more than one woman in a club tossing a romantic glance at Pierre.

But the best indicator that Pierre is, indeed, good looking came from multiply attested experiences that we had in Jerusalem bars. One day, we heard about nice bars in the Russian Compound area. This area is fairly centrally located in Jerusalem. Right near the city center where all the shops and restaurants are. Perhaps, one can say that it is about equal distance away from the center as Mahaneh Yehudah is, except in the opposite direction. I've heard that the reason that the area is called the Russian Compound is that it is near the Russian Orthodox Church. And, in fact, the beautiful church is located less than a couple blocks away from where all the bars are concentrated. I have heard another explan-ation that since the heavy immigration of Russians from Russia, many have settled in the area and that is the reason why it's called the Russian Compound. It is true that many Russian Jews had immigrated from Russia to Israel in the decade under the Israeli Law of Return that allows those who are born Jewish or have immediate Jewish lineage to come to Israel and obtain Israeli citizenship right away.

But I am somewhat skeptical that the place is called the Russian Compound because of the presence of Russian immigrants. For one, I didn't hear too many people speak Russian in the area, and I know for fact that the church had been there before the immigration.

If anything, one heard Yiddish more frequently as there is an ultra religious community in Jerusalem nearby that values Yiddish as a spoken language and considers Hebrew as the elevated religious language. I have heard some secular Israelis complain about these people dressed in black, who were taking all their tax money from the Israeli government. In fact, in modern Hebrew, they are referred to as the Blacks, particularly by the secular Israelis who don't like them. I wonder why people have to attach color to people they don't like. But I guess that's a question for another time.

Going back to the story of bar experiences at the Russian Compound, Pierre and I made our first pilgrimage to the area, one evening. We made our first survey walk throughout the concentrated bar area and tried to decide which one would be the best place for us to be introduced to the culture of the Russian Compound bar scene. Our criteria were quite simple. Decor. Music. And women. Pierre appreciates Rock 'n Roll, so he said that he would want a place with his type of music. Of course, being the accommodating person that I am, I agreed. But I did put my foot down and said that place with great music without beautiful women would be out of the question. Pierre eagerly agreed. With these two criteria clearly delineated, we searched for our bar. There was really only one choice, however, in terms of music. Only one place played all Rock 'n Roll. And fortunately, it also seemed to have a nice concentration of beautiful women.

The decor was horrible, however. It was brightly lit. What was with that? But we were satisfied that there was the fulfillment of at least two out of three criteria, so we decided to hop inside. The place was not totally full, yet. We were to find out later that eleven PM was still pretty early. But our early arrival afforded us the chance to grab the best seats in the room. And that we did. We grabbed the corner table, where we would not be very conspicuous, but we had a clear view of the whole room. The table was facing the television screen which played music videos.

We both ordered a Maccabee beer and some french fries. We were a bit hungry and beer with french fries seemed like the going combination in these parts. But they don't call them french fries, here. They are referred to as chips -- perhaps, a remnant of their English days several decades ago. With the advent of McDonald's, I think french fries as a term will gain more common usage among the Israeli populace. But when we made our visit to the Russian Compound bar, that certainly was not the case. As Pierre and I sat and sipped our Maccabee, named after the national heroes of

Israel during the late Second Temple period, which is roughly equivalent to the period of the Late Antiquity, we weren't sure if we felt like Maccabee the conqueror or not. We felt a little bit out of place, there. Perhaps, it's because both Pierre and I were not used to the bar scene. Perhaps, it's because the place was just too brightly lit for a bar. Anyhow, good music and good music videos made up for the lack of what we considered a classy decor.

There we were, Pierre and I, sipping our Maccabee beers. As always, we did not run out of subjects to talk about. Our individual experiences of the day and our general perception of our collective experience in the new country occupied our conversation. As we became wrapped up in our conversation, we felt a foreign presence near by. It was a young beautiful woman holding a flower in one hand and with other hand holding a basket full of same beautiful singly wrapped flowers. Both Pierre and I thought that she wanted us to purchase the flower, so we simultaneously said, no thank you, in modern Hebrew. We were both beginners in modern Hebrew conversation, but we knew at least that much. The young woman seemed to be puzzled. Then, she smiled and said in English that the flower was for Pierre.

Now, we were puzzled. She must have understood how we could be confused. The young woman quickly added that the flower was from the woman sitting all the way across the room, sitting over there. She pointed while speaking in her surprisingly fluent English. Both Pierre and I looked over at the object of the finger pointing. There, about three tables away, sat a beautiful Israeli woman with her friend. She looked like she was in her early twenties. Pierre was quite surprised. Who could blame him? How many guys ever had a flower sent over by a beautiful woman-stranger? It was obvious that Pierre was quite happy with this situation, and he gave the beautiful woman across the room a friendly nod of his head.

Then, a more bizarre thing happened. At least, bizarre, from the perspective that I had never seen or heard of anything like this before. The young, beautiful woman took out her camera. And, then, I noticed the lens lengthening in what was obviously a zooming in function of the camera. The flash was inaudibly sounded, and the picture of Pierre taken. Wow. That was the only thought that was going through my mind. I wouldn't be surprised if the same word was resounding in Pierre's mind.

I thought this was a good indication that the beautiful woman wanted to meet Pierre. I nudged Pierre and said that we should go over and say, hello. Perhaps, he was taken aback by the whole situation or, maybe, he was embarrassed by the attention that he was getting from the beautiful woman, and, apparently, the whole room. He hesitated. I remembered another of mom's sayings: He who hesitates is lost. I didn't want my friend to lose. I wanted Pierre to win. So, I goaded Pierre, and we walked over to her table.

It was like we were expected. The beautiful woman and her friend were sitting by a square table with two empty chairs. We exchanged our simple pleasantries and names. Pierre and Samuel. Hagit and Dorit. Celebration and Gift, in English translation. I love the way Israeli names often have meanings. We found out that they were actually 19 years old, and they were just about to head on down to Eilat, all the way down south of Israel, to return to the military base where they were serving their two year mandatory military service for women. Women serve from the age of eighteen to twenty and guys serve from eighteen to twenty-one.

Hagit, the one who had sent Pierre the flower and had taken the picture, said that she wanted to see Pierre again when she returns to Jerusalem in several weeks. Hagit said to me into my ear when Pierre was talking with Dorit that she found Pierre very beautiful and that's why she had taken Pierre's picture. Certainly, Hagit was little embarrassed to tell this directly to Pierre. Perhaps, Hagit wanted to make sure the message was clear and reached Pierre through me, especially since Pierre did not broach the topic. We exchanged contact information and tentatively agreed that all of us would have a reunion when they return back. I felt bad for Pierre because he seemed attracted to Hagit and vice versa. After they left to drive all night long to their military base down south, Pierre said, damn the military. It's the first time I heard this from him, since he was quite proud of the Israeli military and, quite frequently, talked about how neat it would be to serve in it.

As surprising as this case of a beautiful woman taking a photo of Pierre was, it was not to be an isolated case. It happened two more times. Granted they were not as beautiful as Hagit; she looked like a model out of a cover page of *Elle*. I wouldn't be surprised if I see her in a magazine or hear about her rise to fame due to her feminine beauty in the future. The other two were both quite attractive young Israeli women, one in her early twenties and the other one in her mid-twenties. Both times, however, it was just taking of the photo but no flower. But both times, the women remarked about how beautiful they thought Pierre was. Perhaps, Pierre should look into being a male model. Maybe, Pierre and Hagit can appear together as supermodels in a magazine.

Although I can't fully appreciate what the three picture taking beautiful women saw in Pierre as I am generally used to appreciating the beauty of women, I fully understand that women find him attractive. It would not be surprising if the women at the Jerusalem market found pleasure in seeing him shop the way guys found pleasure in seeing some beautiful Israeli women shopping. Pierre, I know, would not be displeased to provide this service.

With Pierre's love for the culinary experience and my enjoyment of the whole shopping experience, we set out to get what we needed for the feast that we were going to throw for Orit and Orli. It was quite easy this time as we had a clear shopping list of what we wanted to buy. We also had a sense of purpose.

Perhaps, it was this sense of mission that the shopping was for the sake of a greater ideal or goal that made this shopping experience a little bit more mechanical than our previous trips. We knew what we wanted and why we wanted it. In the previous shopping ex-periences, we were often quite open to possibilities. Sure, in every shopping excursion we knew that there were certain things we absolutely needed, such as salt or oil when they ran out. However, much else was open to the spirit of the market place. We wandered through Mahaneh Yehudah looking for what we might want in the same way a child would joyously wander through a toy store, open to all possibilities. Often, the discussion regarding what to get and what we would make with what we were going to get was open. I wouldn't be surprised if I were told that our colorful discussions on the food matter attracted interest away from fellow shoppers, more than a few times.

This time, there were no such discussions. Food discussions were concluded yesterday in our apartment. We knew that we were there in the shopping place for a purpose. We were focused on the Operation Food Know dinner at our little humble abode, and that made this particular shopping experience somewhat mechanical. We picked up the items that we needed and before we knew it, we were heading back to the bus stop at the center of town with our backpacks full of food.

4

Cook Galore

Now, the mission was to make food even good enough for heavenly palates. The dessert is often the most important part of the meal, and in our case it was the most difficult part as well. Pierre was going to make chocolate mousse. It was the perfect dessert to wind down the meal. Who doesn't like chocolate? I did not observe Pierre making the chocolate mousse attentively as I should have, but I came away with one distinct impression. It is very difficult to make chocolate mousse. I'll describe what I saw as best as I remember it.

The two essential ingredients, as I understand it, are chocolate and eggs. Pierre had brought several chocolate bars from France. Pierre loved French chocolate, and he told me that he never traveled outside of his country without a good supply of them. Pierre took one of these concentrated chocolate bars and said that he was going to use this great French chocolate to make an extraordinary chocolate mousse. No complaints, certainly from my corner. But before he did anything with the chocolate, Pierre said that he had to do something with the egg. He took out a piece of paper, on which he scribbled down instructions from his mom regarding how to make the best French chocolate mousse this side of France. The first and most difficult process was to isolate the white part of the egg, beat it, and make a form of whipped cream out of it. The question was how. We didn't have an egg beater. We were stocked with just simple utensils of knives, forks, and spoons. Pierre decided that he would use a spoon to beat the egg white.

The way he went about isolating the egg white was kind of artistic, I thought. He broke the egg shells into about equal halves. And it was so neatly done; I don't think I could ever do that. Whenever I tried to crack open eggs, it's never a clear cut. Around the point of impact of an external object, pieces of egg shells seem to crumble and even fall into the flying pan, when I want to make eggs over-and-easy. More than once, I burned my fingers trying to fish out the small egg shell pieces. But with Pierre, it was different. The first egg that he cracked open had two beautifully halved shells. It was the case with every other egg that he halved. I watched as he elevated one half containing the yolk over the half containing some white part of the egg. Then, he dumped the yolk from the elevated half to the lowered half. And he reversed the process, elevating the egg half containing the yolk and lowering the half formerly containing the yolk. Then, he repeated the process. He poured yolk from the elevated half to the lowered half. He did this over and over again. Soon, I was looking at a half eggshell containing the yolk and the other half containing the white. Behind the two halves I could see the big smile on Pierre's face. After repeating this process a few times with several eggs, all of them being cracked open in a nice smooth cut into halves, Pierre held a bowl containing a significant amount of egg whites.

Now came the hard part, Pierre said. He held a spoon with his right hand and the bowl with his left hand. Then, Pierre proceeded to make a circular motion with the spoon. The bowl was held about half a foot away from Pierre's face and the circular motion of the spoon revolved around a central point little bit above the egg white mass. The revolving radius of the motion around the central point involved diving into the white egg mass and then moving away from the white egg mass and toward Pierre's face. Once, Pierre jerked his motion accidentally and had a bit of the white egg mass spattered on his face. The expected expletive was absent; rather, he smiled out loud. Perhaps, it gave Pierre pleasure to be making something for beautiful women. I noticed a big smile on his face whenever we passed by beautiful women, and the smile he had on at that moment was not so different from that.

Or, perhaps, Pierre was enjoying making a proud French dish, and it gave him pleasure to be participating in this wonderful

French culture that he felt so integrally a part of. I have often seen a beaming smile whenever Pierre talked about the merits of fine French cuisine. Particularly, when he talked about his favorite restaurant near his house, he would light up with a beaming smile. He talked about the starter, the soup, the main course, and the dessert often in vivid detail. By the end of my being roommates with him after a year, I think I was intricately familiar with everything on the menu of that restaurant. Certainly, after all the preaching regarding the extraordinary nature of the food in the restaurant, I became a convert, eager to make my pilgrimage there, to partake of the wellsprings of celestial French cuisine.

Was it because Pierre was feeling like an instrument of this incredible cuisine, a kind of a messenger -- yes, even an angel -- that brought smiles behind a face spattered with egg whites? Whatever might have been the reason for the smile, Pierre did not pause to give an explanation. Pierre gave me a simple direct smile, almost an afterthought, and proceeded in his concentrated task. The egg beating went on for about thirty minutes. I didn't clock it or anything but I felt after spending time memorizing some modern Hebrew vocabulary, that's about how much time that had passed. I figured, there was not much that I could do to help at that point in the preparation of chocolate mousse.

And I thought learning modern Hebrew vocabulary might come in handy for both of us. After all, we didn't know how fluent Orli was in English. She might not be as fluent as Orit. Even knowing a few more words and using them could make Orli more comfortable and the whole evening that much more pleasant. Especially since I was charged with the social aspects of our dinner invitations, I felt a sense of duty. Somehow, this time, memorizing modern Hebrew vocabulary seemed little more fun than other times. In fact, I was so concentrated on my task at hand, I didn't see all that Pierre did with the chocolate and the beaten egg whites. Pierre said that now he was ready to put the whole thing in the freezer, and it should be ready by tomorrow night, when the guests arrive. Rest of the food, we were going to make tomorrow, a few hours before their arrival.

The well-fated evening came early enough. Much of our intermittent conversation before the main event concerned how Orli might look. We were admittedly a little bit nervous because this was going to be our first dinner with Israeli women in Operation Food Know our project of mutual understanding and good will. Okay, perhaps, we wanted a little bit more than that. But we didn't know exactly what to expect. First of all, being fairly new to this country and city, Pierre and I were not sure how our Frenchness and Americanness would come across. We were hoping that we wouldn't do anything to offend Orit and Orli. But on the other hand, we didn't want our behavior to be unnatural. We should be our natural selves. Isn't this the way one really comes to know someone, when one behaves the way that one normally does?

Since we were dealing with women, the situation seemed to be more complicated. I invited Orit and her friend Orli in a friendly way. How did Orit make of this? What were they saying to each other? Is it normal for two single guys to invite women like this in Israeli culture? Were they thinking of this as a friendly dinner, or were they thinking of this dinner as something more? Like a double date? Will they expect us to make some kind of romantic gestures? There was just a ple-thora of questions that were running through my mind, and from my conversation with Pierre, it seemed that he was having a vicarious experience. I decided that I was just going to be myself and be friendly and let the dinner take its course. I was certainly attracted to Orit, but I was not planning to make any efforts for romance. It's better just to plan to get to know each other better. Maybe, she would want to have me just as a friend. I might feel the same way after getting to know her better, although I doubted it, highly. This certainly was a good course of action. Everyone just gets to know each other better without any expectations.

Some of these thoughts were still going through my mind as I prepared my dish. It wasn't such a hard dish to prepare. Fried vegetables. I cracked open several eggs. I did not need neatly divided halves, and I was fortunate since as usual my egg halves were not neatly divided. I had to peel off some small broken pieces tenuously holding onto the halves. Afterwards, I just dumped the contents inside the egg shells, whites and yoke and all, into a bowl. I repeated this action, more or less in the same way, with two more eggs. Now, I had three eggs inside a bowl.

I broke the yolk circles and watched the yellow color make their way into the whites of the egg. I helped their journey along by providing a whirling motion with a fork. Soon enough, I had a nice mixed egg paste inside a small bowl. I, then, broke open the bag of flour that I had purchased the day before in the Jerusalem market place. Now, some of the important components were ready.

I needed to get the vegetables ready, as well. This wasn't too difficult either. I got some carrots, peeled their skin, and cut them into small pieces. I took some potatoes, peeled their skin, and cut them into small pieces. I grabbed some zucchini and cut them into small pieces. I didn't peel the skin because I remembered that mom did not do that with zucchini. I put all the cut up vegetable pieces into a bowl, somewhat bigger than the bowl containing the egg mixture. Then, I grabbed another bowl, about the same size with the vegetable bowl and put about one fourth of the flour from the flour bag containing words completely in modern Hebrew. I put the flour bag away, and, then, I reached for a skillet frying pan and placed it on top of the gas stove. I turned the gas stove on and applied a lighted match from the Hyatt Regency Hotel match box that mom gave me before I left for Israel. She had picked it up from Hyatt Regency Hotel in Jerusalem during her visit the year before my visit to Israel. I guess it was a way of wishing me luck. I noticed that the matches were almost gone. It's a surprise that it lasted this long. After all, I was several weeks into my stay in Jerusalem and the gas stove required matches every time to light it.

After the gas stove was ready and the frying pan was beginning to warm on top of it, I looked for the vegetable oil that I had purchased when I bought the bag of flour. We had olive oil, but I liked to use it for salads and certain kinds of cooking. Also, olive oil was more expensive than the generic vegetable oil.

Since I needed to use a lot of oil for my fried vegetables, I wanted to conserve the precious olive oil. Pierre must have placed the vegetable oil in a different location. It didn't take long for me to find, however, as our kitchen was quite small. There were only three semi-large kitchen cabinets, so I knew that the vegetable oil had to be in one of these. I saw Pierre vigorous preparing his honey glazed chicken, so I didn't want to break his concentration. It seemed like a serious project with him.

Sure enough, the vegetable oil was right inside the next cabinet door that I opened. I applied generous amounts of vegetable oil inside the frying pan, enough so that the vegetables could almost swim in it. Certainly, when dunked inside the vegetable oil, their bodies were at least half covered with oil. I could afford to flip them over once, but I didn't want to do more than that. I felt the vegetable oil warming up. I dipped my washed left hand onto the vegetable dish and grabbed a few vegetables, and, then, I dipped them on the egg mixture. Then came the fun part. I dipped the egg-greased vegetables on the flour bowl, and from there they came out covered with white flour all over. I then proceeded to place the newly clothed vegetables into the now hot oil pool. As the vegetables entered the large body of oil liquid, they simmered. White flour turned quickly into almost a golden yellow color.

As I predicted, the bunched-together vegetables were too much for the height of the oil pool. Their top stuck out, and that part of the vegetables stayed white. I wanted to give that side also a nice cookover, so I turned the vegetables over after about a minute. It took only about two minutes for the vegetables to be cooked and ready. I repeated this, and after about thirty minutes, I had a batch more than aplenty for four people. We will probably have some left over and be able to eat them for lunch, tomorrow, I remember thinking to myself, then.

I looked over to where Pierre was making his honey glazed chicken. He had already applied honey onto the chicken and added some other spices on top. He had the piece of paper next to him containing directions that he got from his mom. I could see itemized recipes in French -- one for the chocolate mousse and the other one for the honey glazed chicken -- all on that one piece of paper. He had some sliced almonds in a small bag that he picked up at Mahaneh Yehudah when we went shopping, the day before, for this momentous dinner. Pierre sprinkled the almond pieces generously onto the honey glazed chicken. I thought that was a nice touch. Even before the chicken was cooked, it looked aesthetically pleasing and almost appetizing.

Pierre put five honey glazed chicken pieces onto a pan and placed it inside the portable oven that we had purchased at the beginning of our stay together in the apartment. The apartment did not come with an oven. At first, we thought we would not need an oven, but we saw a good deal for a used oven slash toaster that a student who was leaving to go back home to the United States was selling, so we decided to purchase it. I like my bread toasted once in a while, so even if we didn't use the oven, I figured that I could use it to toast my bread. Looking at Pierre placing honey glazed chicken pieces inside that portable oven, I felt lucky that Pierre and I had purchased that portable oven. Pierre's glazed chicken will be done in a little while, and my fried vegetable appetizer was already complete.

Pierre paused what he was doing and wondered out loud about how the chocolate mousse turned out. He opened the freezer and looked at the bowl containing his hard work from the day before. Pierre did not emerge from the examination with big smiles that I was expecting. I asked him, what was wrong. Pierre said that the mousse looked nothing like the mousse that his mother makes. It looked a little soft, and it's supposed to be solid. I asked to have a look, and to my eyes, it looked just fine. And the smell, it was simply out of this world. Perhaps, Pierre was right about the importance of using only French chocolate for the chocolate mousse. I told him that it looked fine and that the ladies would love it. Pierre seemed somewhat mollified. I reassured him, you'll see. They'll love it!

We knew what we needed to do next. There was considerable mess created in the wake of our culinary creations. The apartment had to look spotless before the two Israeli beauties graced our threshold. Pierre grabbed a mop, and I took the sponge. I soaked the sponge in liquid soap and proceeded to clean the top of the stove and the table where we were to share our friendship meal. Pierre did a swift but thorough job cleaning the floor of our apartment. After we did each of our prospective roles in making the place clean enough for two guests whose opinions about us might, at least, be partly formed by how our apartment looks, we had the obligation of making ourselves look pretty, remaining. We tossed a coin to see who was going to take a shower first. Heads. Pierre would take the shower first, and, then, I would follow. Pierre was pretty good about taking a short shower, so it wasn't a problem.

5

Space Continuum

This was it. The final stretch before our monumental dinner of cross-cultural exchange and international fellowship with hope of something more. As Pierre was taking his shower, I took a moment's pause, sitting on my bed. Here, I was in a country quite different from what I was used to with a roommate from a country that had a different culture from mine, ready to have guests from the host country. It's almost ironic that our first friendship dinner was one in which, we, the guests to this country, were playing the host. I had not thought of it in such terms until that moment, sitting on the bed.

I remember looking around the room and realizing how small the room was. There were two beds, one on each side of the room, and the beds were separated basically by two desks placed side by side facing the window. The desks were not too big. I would say that they were comparable in the desk category to the single beds that Pierre and I had, which were the lowest in the bed category. The desks were sufficient enough for study but not so big that one could put a whole pile of books or create an artificial single row bookshelf on it. These moderately sized desks placed side by side were practically touching our single beds that were at the sides of the room. The beds were pushed vertically right up to the side of the wall with the windows -- the side that faced the entrance way into the room from the small dining room area. At the opposite vertical end, the beds were separated by only about one foot from the side of the room with the door, which faced directly towards the windows. In reality, there were about two feet from the bottom of the bed to the side of the wall with the door. But practically, there was only one foot of open space, since there were large singular cabinets containing drawers and smaller cabinet compartments within that stuck to the either side of the wall next to the door. That's where Pierre and I put our clothes. Real open space was in the middle of the room composed of less than seven feet by seven feet. In positive terms, it was a very cozy room. Perhaps, the smallness of the size of the room helped Pierre and me to bond better. It's good that Pierre and I got along. Can you imagine if you didn't get along with your roommate? I was asking myself this question as I looked out through the opened doorway to the dining room.

Perhaps, the word dining room is not the most accurate term to describe the small space with a dining room table. The space was so small that the table had to be pushed against the wall by its long side to allow us to walk around it. Walking around it was a necessity because the long side of the wall that contained a window in the corner on the right side directly faced the front door of the apartment, the entry point from the outside world. Even with the long side of the table pushed to the side of the wall, there were hardly two to three steps between the door to the apartment and the immediate long side of the table. That was not all. One shorter side of the table was only about two steps from the door to our room. How about the other short side? It faced the gas stove with four burners. The gas stove in a square formation was a part of one kitchen set that included a sink, which was right next to it. The sink was right next to a small, open, connected table space where we placed the portable oven. The outer edge of the portable oven was placed neatly to match the end of the single table unit. Right next to that was a refrigerator. The refrigerator was a fairly decent sized one and pretty new. I wondered how they got the refrigerator in there, since there seemed to be hardly any room to move the refrigerator that was pressing against the walls on two sides and the singular kitchen unit on its other side. When Pierre or I opened the refrigerator door, it didn't even open fully because there was a wall about a step away from the front side of the refrigerator.

The area, which could be more properly termed, kitchen-dining room-threshold-in-one was not neatly rectangular in shape. The front door was at a protrusion. I didn't quite understand the practicality of this from the perspective of one living inside the apartment. I decided to check it out from the outside. I had never paid serious attention to how it looked from the outside and now was as good a time as ever to try to see what practicality the architects had in mind. So, I got up from my bed, walked through the small door way, and, already, I was holding the door knob to go out of the apartment. I went out and closed the door. I didn't have to worry about being locked out because all locks were engaged manually. To open the door, one had to insert the key from the outside or the inside. To lock the door, one needed a key to do so on either side of the door.

If one stuck a key from the inside after locking the door and left it there, a person from the outside would not be able to stick his key in to open the door. Pierre had once done this when talking on the cordless phone that he liked so much. He must have just walked in and started talking on the phone, since he almost never just left the key inside the door. In this particular occasion, it was a bit embarrassing for me because I walked home with a cute Argentinean student who was studying at the university who happened to live nearby. She had expressed interest in seeing my pictures from the US. When I tried to insert my key into the apartment door to open it, I wasn't able to do that. Since I did not fully understand the mechanics of the way the door lock system worked at that time, I kept trying to insert my key in. I even started to talk to myself, then, quickly caught myself, and faced Christina, so as not to freak her out. I told her and myself, how strange it was that my key wasn't working. I might even have started to perspire a little bit. It was pretty hot outside, in the high 80 degrees and the situation did not help any.

What made it worse was that Christina thought I was kidding. She smiled and told me not to joke around any more. Then, I was clueless as to what was going on with the key. So, hoping that Pierre was inside, I rang the doorbell. I heard Pierre's footsteps and in a very short while, the door was opened. I quickly caught myself and introduced Pierre to the lovely Christina. The story had a semi happy ending, at least for that day, in that Christina enjoyed watching the photos and left smiling. I think that short, humorous captions that I wrote next to the pictures helped her forget about the door incident. But who knows? Maybe she went back to her apartment and discussed with her roommates about the weird incident by the doorway to Samuel's apartment. Mom used to say, Experience is the best teacher. This experience at least taught me and Pierre the intricate workings of our

apartment's lock system. It's funny how standing outside the apartment door brought that
memory back.

I, now, looked at my apartment door
that was closed. There was an indent leading
to the door way. The bell was at the right side
of the wall. Actually, the little indentation
could not accommodate more than two people.
Maybe three very skinny people. I realized
that the indented wall with the door bell was
the flip-side of the wall that was facing the
refrigerator. I turned around to see if this
indentation was necessary. In fact, it was.
When I turned around 180 degrees, I saw a flat,
small space with stairs going up on my left
side. Directly in front of me was a space of
about five steps and after about four steps,
there was a slight indentation to the right that
led to the doorway to my next door neighbor.
The walkway from my apartment to my
neighbor's could not have accommodated three
people if they were walking side by side. I
didn't think about it before, but I realized how
small the walkway was. And parallel to the
stairs going up right next to my apartment was
a stairway that was going down. This stairway
actually directly faced the doorway of my
neighbor's apartment doorway. There were
only two apartments on our floor. There was a
small open space between the parallel stair-
ways that went down and up. I looked down

through the crevice and was able to see about three more levels down. I looked up and could see about seven more levels upwards. There was no worry about people falling into this small crevice. It was too small for any one to really fit inside. Wow, this place was pretty small.

I heard the voice of Pierre, proclaiming loudly that he was done with shower. I guess that was his way of calling me when he didn't find me in the room. I took a few steps, opened the apartment door, thanked him for letting me know, and walked past the dining table towards the shower. I was so space conscious by then, that I wanted to see how the rest of the apartment was like as I walked towards the shower room. The outer edge of the dining table that faced the doorway into my and Pierre's room provided the linear continuation of the wall of the hallway leading to the shower room. The long side of the dining room table was pushed against the wall that was perpendicular to the wall of the hallway. The hallway itself was pretty narrow, hardly two steps wide.

In the spirit of measurement, I made sure that I counted my steps as I walked towards the end of the hallway. After two steps, there was, to the right, a doorway that led to a small room with a toilette -- just the toilet. It was a little bit bigger than the airplane toilettes. Despite the small size, I did think that the toilette room was highly practical. It was in a separate room, so if one needed to go about relieving oneself, that would not hold up someone who may need to take a shower or freshen up in the morning. But I thought that it would not be a bad idea to have a little sink in the toilette room, so that one could wash one's hands after relieving oneself. If I ever meet the designer of this apartment, I would be sure to mention that.

Pierre likes to lock his shower room door when he takes his shower, and there have been more than one occasion, in which I waited for him to come out in order to wash my hands. Sure, I could have walked over to the kitchen sink to wash my hands, but that seemed, somehow, not to be a right thing to do. In a way, I felt I was bringing in something profane to the sacred space of food, cooking, and eating. I understand the impracticality of this thought since, in terms of space, the toilette was right against the wall which the long side of our dining table was intimately touching.

I wanted to dispel this unpleasant thought from my mind, so I took two more steps. Directly in front of me was a dead end. I have to remember to put up a poster or something. It's just a bland wall without anything on it. To the left was the door to another room, not unlike the one that Pierre and I were occupying. Directly in front of the door to that room was the door that led to the shower room.

The door was already open and I was able to feel the warm mist from the previous shower. It's always more pleasant to take the shower first, I remember thinking. There was about one and a half steps from the opening of the door to the facing wall. In fact, the door hardly opened full way. It was like a small corridor, inside. After entering the small room, I purposefully made a perpendicular turn. One step afterwards, there was a sink to my left with a small mirror. And one step later, there was the glass door to the shower. A very small cubicle that could only barely fit in one person. Having taken my clothes off and turned on the water to my liking, in terms of temperature and pressure, I started to soap myself. I realized that the space was so small that it was even difficult to bend all the way down to wash my feet. I found myself having to raise my feet and meet my hand with soap half way.

Often, showers tend to be mechanical. Especially in the morning, I don't think I have a singular thought in my mind as I take my shower. But this time, I felt that even taking a shower was deliberate. Perhaps, it's partly due to my consciousness about space that, some-how, started during the short pause after cooking, only moments before. Perhaps, it's due in part to the anticipation of seeing the beautiful Orit, again. Ah, Orit the Beautiful. She looked so stunningly attractive in that uniform. It was kind of loose on her, but in tight areas, I could see her distinctively attractive feminine form. I realized that I was taking a little bit more time than I usually did during my morning showers, so I stopped myself from continuing my mental journey down the beautiful lane. After all, I would see her in person, soon enough. And we were running out of time. I quickly washed my hair with my favorite shampoo, Finesse. I rinsed off, and I felt better than new. Now, the question was what I was going to wear.

6

The Blue Dude

It's not too difficult deciding what to wear, one would think. Just throw on a shirt and jeans. Casual would be good. With this thought I hurried back to my room. Not having a watch on me, I wasn't sure how I was doing on time. When I entered the room, the first thing I noticed was how dressed up Pierre was. Pierre was wearing a yellow dress shirt. It looked new from the neatly pressed lines that seemed so symmetric. Perhaps, Pierre was saving this beautiful shirt for such an occasion, when two beautiful women were going to grace our apartment. And his pants could definitely qualify as a dress pants. It wasn't new, as one could tell from the fact that the creases were not so even and neat. It was obvious that Pierre tried to press the pants himself. But it was classy pants.

As if reading the questions on my face, Pierre replied that it was the first major dinner in Jerusalem, and such a momentous occasion required a special dress. It sure was a special occasion, but I remembered what one of my newly made Israeli friends told me. Oren told me that his beloved prime minister Itzak Rabin almost never wore a tie. Even in formal occasions, he would wear a plain shirt and pants. Oren said that this might indicate why many Israelis loved Rabin. He was the embodiment of the Israeli Every Man. So, taking Oren's statement at face value, I asked

Pierre, if he realized that he was really dressed up by Israeli standards. Pierre retorted with a puzzled look. I explained to him the conversation that I had with Oren.

Pierre knew who Oren was because Oren had stopped by our apartment several days ago. He was interested in seeing my CD collection. I had brought a portable CD player with about twelve CD's. Among my collection of CD's was *The Phantom of the Opera* soundtrack. When I told him that, he said that he had to hear it. Apparently, he had seen *The Phantom* in London. It was the first international city that he visited, Oren told me. It was right after the army. He worked six months down in Eilat at one of the hotels to raise money to make the almost obligatory after-the-army trip that many Israelis make. One of the popular destinations is the Far East. I noticed quite a number of Israelis included South-East Asia and India in this category as well as Australia and New Zealand. And it was this destination that Oren worked so hard to visit. In the course of working six months in Eilat, Oren managed to raise several thousand dollars. So, he bought a discounted airline ticket and had about four thousand dollars of spending money. It sounds a lot but Oren was going to spend that over the period of six months. That was the plan, Oren said. Before heading to the Far East, Oren wanted to make a short stop in England. And this was quite easy since he was flying British Airways, and London is one of their hub cities. So, Oren was able to have a free stopover.

Oren found out that this was about the only thing that was free. Apparently, Oren did not accurately calculate how much it was going to cost him to stay in London. Oren had planned to stay one week in London and explore as much as he could. But Oren made the mistake of starting his trip in August, which is a high tourist season in London. It was the first time he was traveling out of the country, so Oren did not blame himself too much. Oren decided just to bite the bullet. Since he had made no previous lodging arrangements and was new to the city, he ended up finding a pretty expensive lodging, which was about seven times what he was expecting to pay. And since the monetary denominations were lower, something like one Pound to about six New Israeli Shekels, the expensive cost of lodging and other things, such as food, did not immediately register in Oren's mind.

Thinking, when else would he have the opportunity to stay in London for one week, Oren hit all the sites, whose entrance fees were not cheap. Since he was right out of the army and this trip was before his university studies, Oren had no student ID card and did not even think about finding a way to obtain an international student card or discount card of some sort.

Being over twenty-one, Oren paid adult price for everything. Despite paying and then paying some more, Oren remembered his seven days in London with fondness. The highlight for him was seeing the performance of *The Phantom of the Opera*. He even brought pictures to show himself in front of the theater.

I noticed that there was a beautiful blonde woman standing next to him. This, of course, begged the question regarding who she was. Oren admitted that he went to the theater with her. Oren met her in the place of his lodging. He was traveling alone and she was traveling alone. He met her in the TV room in the basement, the first night of his arrival. She was watching *Bay Watch* on TV, and since it was Oren's favorite show, or immediately became his favorite show after about five minutes, he joined her. They were the only ones in the room and the conversation naturally started.

He told her that he was from Israel and had recently finished his military service. The girl turned out to be American and from Wisconsin. She had just graduated from the University of Wisconsin at Madison and was traveling with friends through Europe. But all of her friends wanted to stay in Paris several more days, so she had come to London alone. I noticed she was really beautiful in the picture and told Oren, so. Oren told me that she was not always that way. Lorilee had shown him a picture of herself from high school days. She was quite overweight. Lorilee had lost one hundred fifty pounds in college. It was an impressive achievement and Oren told her that she had every right to be proud of herself. This frank compliment had warmed Lorilee's heart, and she opened up to Oren. Lorilee told Oren about the difficulties that she was still experiencing trying to keep the weight off. Lorilee exercised two hours every day and without fail. Lorilee shared more with Oren than just her exercise routine.

After an hour's conversation, Lorilee told Oren that when she first saw him ogling at the Bay Watch babes, she had thought of him as a typical guy, but she was pleasantly surprised and happy to see that he's a sensitive guy. Soon after she said that, Lorilee asked Oren if he's ever seen a musical. Oren had never seen a musical. Lorilee told Oren that it would be sin not to see at least one musical while being in London, so they agreed to go see a musical next night. Lorilee had an appointment to visit her mother's sister's friend in London, this night, so she was going to fulfill her obligation to her aunt. Promise was a promise, after all.

The next day, Oren woke up a little late, perhaps due to jet lag. Most likely, it was due to staying up all night talking to his army buddies before the big trip that had fatigued him so much. Oren woke up in time for lunch and just grabbed something from around the corner. When he got back, he visited Lorilee's room to see if she were there. There was a note for him saying that she was out exercising for two hours and would like to meet up with him at five o' clock. Oren liked to walk, so he decided to take the address of where he was staying and a simple map from the front desk and explore the neighborhood where he found himself.

Oren purposely allowed himself to get lost. He had some four hours to kill, and, besides, exploring the streets of London was pretty neat. British architecture was quite different from Israel's, and everything seemed kind of exotic, Oren recounted. Perhaps, that put Oren in a little romantic mood. By the time that five o' clock came around, Oren was very excited and looking forward to seeing Lorilee as much as he was looking forward to seeing his first musical. They decided on *The Phantom of the Opera*. Oren said that it was the most romantic atmosphere he experienced in his life, so far. During one of the more romantic musical scores, Oren said that he reached over and held Lorilee's hand. Lorilee looked over to

Oren and just smiled and then turned to continue seeing the musical. Oren was excited by this sweet, yet innocent, gesture and kept holding her hand. And that's all that happened throughout the musical. Oren held her hand.

After the theater performance, Oren and Lorilee decided to go dancing at a nearby club. They both enjoyed dancing. And it was at this club, that Oren first kissed Lorilee. Oren did not remember the details of the club. Oren said that he remembered holding Lorilee and kissing her. Oren said, the rest is history. So I asked him, what that history was. Oren spent rest of the week with Lorilee in London. Lorilee rearranged her ticket so that she could fly out of London on the same day that Oren was planning to. Apparently, Oren wrote to Lorilee from everywhere he went after that.

Lorilee decided that she would come to work in Israel for a while when Oren was scheduled to arrive back to Israel after six months, so Lorilee looked for work. With her education, she was able to get a good job, easily. She was hired with Andersen Consulting in Tel Aviv. In fact, she was living there right now. Since he was studying at the university in Jerusalem, Oren was living in Jerusalem. But Oren left every Thursday, which is equivalent to American Friday, for Tel Aviv for the whole weekend. Since Oren did not have classes on Sunday, which is equivalent to the American Monday, he came back on Sunday night to Jerusalem. They were just as much in love now if not more, Oren added. When he told me this, I was compelled to give him the disk of *The Phantom of the Opera* as a gift.

Pierre found the story very romantic and wished Oren the best. But for some reason, Pierre did not like Oren very much. I don't know why. Oren was a very nice guy, I thought. It might be because Oren only stopped by in London and not in Paris. Pierre was very proud of his city. Also, Oren made a couple of jokes about France. One of the things he said was that in England they refer to condoms as French letters. Is that kind of like referring to chips as French fries in the USA? Anyhow, other jokes seemed more harmless than the first one. But, perhaps, the combination of Oren not stopping by Paris and the jokes about France might have been too much for Pierre. Despite the fact that Pierre did not like Oren very much, my mention of his name this time did not seem to have an adverse effect on Pierre. In fact, Pierre said that what Oren said about Prime Minister Rabin and his clothing was pretty interesting. But Pierre did add that he was a Frenchman and he was going to look nice for the ladies in the French way. I did not want to pursue the topic or make a conversation out of his statement, so I replied that I would dress similarly as well.

Mom had packed me a nice dress shirt that I bought at the Izod outlet store in Reading, Pennsylvania. It's true that the price was quite hard to beat. It must have been fully one third of the price that I remember seeing at the department stores. Mom recommended the color and I liked it so I agreed to the purchase. It was a light blue color. It wasn't one of those deep sea blue colors which makes you feel like you are about to drown. And it wasn't one of those overcast sky blue colors which forebodes depressing things for the future. Rather, it was a bright, light blue color that was full of hope.

Mom and dad liked to take us kids to Reading on these annual outings. There were some good smorgasbords, as well. Dad really liked all-you-can-eat traditional American cuisine restaurants. And mom made sure that we stopped by some outlet stores, since Reading is the East Coast capital of outlet stores. It would be wrong not to make a few stops. I don't think we are the only family with frequent shopping-buffet tours in Reading. More than a few friends admitted to such a family outing. Many of my male friends, at first, seemed embarrassed to admit to it, but as time went on and we grew older, the truth came out. And some even had a sense of pride recounting one of their family traditions.

I had the shirt in hand: so now, I had to pick out my pants. I thought that blue on blue would be good. They can call me the Blue Dude. I wondered if the term, dude, was common in Israel? I had no matching pants -- at least not of the same color. But I did have dark blue pants. My love of all things blue outweighed my fear at possibly being called the walking sea scenery. Bright blue sky top with a deep sea blue in the bottom. I looked at the mirror. I looked pretty good, actually. In fact, both of us looked good. We were ready for the guests. Food was ready. The apartment was spotless. All the portents were positive.

7

Orit and Orli Visit

The time finally arrived. We heard the door bell ring, and after a few steps, I was opening the door for Orit and Orli. How can I describe how they looked? Let me begin by describing how Orit looked since she was standing in front. The first thing I noticed about her was her smile. She had the same radiant smile that I remembered from several days ago. This time, Orit was not wearing her army uniform or blandishing her M16. She was actually fairly casually dressed. She was wearing a blue shirt with black polka dots and a fairly tight faded blue jeans. I thought that Orit's shirt was particularly disarming. To be frank, I had never seen a shirt like that before in my life. The polka dots added an element of youthful playfulness. And the blue color of the shirt was what I would describe as an optimistic blue. It wasn't sky blue, but it was a clear, solid blue color that was quite pleasant to look at. Of course, one was not necessarily drawn to the blueness of the shirt since it was covered all over with polka dots. Her clothes were quite pleasant to look at especially because they stuck so engagingly to her skin. I had a clearer idea of her feminine form than when I saw her in her army uniform. Fairly loose fit of the army uniform, certainly in comparison to her present outfit, certainly did not do justice to her physical form even with the strong element of male imagination thrown in to the equation. I realized that Orit noticed my checking her over visually, but her smile was ever present in her face. This I took as a positive sign.

I have often asked the question in my mind as I did at that moment albeit only briefly, Why was it that I did not have the gift that Pierre did? He was able to look over a woman and check her out without being noticed. For me, it was, more often than not, that my gazes were noticed. I remember Pierre once telling me that it was not necessarily a good thing to be noticed. Some women do find this flattering, Pierre said, because they realize that the guy finds her attractive. But there is a number of women who finds this somewhat intrusive. I thought that people look at each other, and it goes both ways. Pierre joked that when a guy is looking at a woman, often there's the perception that the guy wants only one thing. Can't a guy just appreciate a woman's beauty in a similar way that, as I have heard, my female friends verbally check out a guy?

Pierre said that it's a gift that he never was noticed while checking out a woman, and it is one of the most important skills that a guy must foster if he is not born with it. Of course, I tried to mount a defensive. In the same way a tennis player blames his racket for a lost point, I offered the possibility that it might be the high level of my astigmatism that required a longer time to focus visually. Lost fractions of seconds gave my visual appreciation away. I'm sure that Pierre was doing the same thing that I did vis-a-vis Orit, but he just wasn't noticed. He did have the advantage of standing behind me as well since I was the one who opened the door.

I was ebullient with my warm greetings toward Orit. Visual stimulation was certainly a contributing factor to my heartfelt and earnest greeting. I introduced Orit to my roommate, Pierre. Pierre uttered a short pleasantry in his polite manner. If Pierre was anything, he was polite. Everybody that got to know him always commented to me that they were impressed with his politeness. One friend asked me if his politeness was a French thing. I didn't know too much about the general French culture and mores to give him a definitive answer to that question. He responded with the comment that he now had to revise his opinion that all French are rude. Apparently, he had a bad experience in France that prompted that perception.

He had been on vacation with his family in Paris for one day in such a stereotypically American fashion. I have often heard jokes from Europeans about how Americans travel through seven countries in seven days. He had been in the Versailles palace and needed to use the bathroom. With the little French that he learned in college -- he only had a couple of semesters of French -- he proceeded to ask where the bathroom was. He knew that the question was grammatically correct, but he realized that his French question was heavy laden with an American accent. Perhaps, this was an element of offense to those French people whom he asked. None of them dignified his question with a response. From his account of the story, he had to ask about six people before getting an answer regarding where the bathroom was.

I told this account to Pierre, and he noted that he was quite surprised by what my friend experienced. Pierre pointed out that most French people that he knew would gladly be of help. Pierre raised the question as to whether they understood the question at all. It's possible that they didn't understand his question. After all, by my friend's own admission, his American accent did impinge on his French. I thought Pierre might have a point there, but, then, my friend did get a response from the sixth person. This shows that he understood him, and if this French person understood him, would it not be safe to assume that at least a couple out of the other four did as well? To this day, the jury is out regarding that particular incident. But it's true that Pierre is extremely polite, so those who know him could not in good conscience say that all French are rude. I told Pierre, two thumbs up for you for breaking stereotypes. Pierre seemed pleased by the small part he was playing in providing a good picture of the French, so he was enthusiastic in his politeness. And, actually, after I pointed this out, Pierre talked more than usual about the merits of French politeness.

However, I thought that it was, at least partly if not mostly, his family upbringing that created the polite Pierre. Pierre came from an upper middle class family. His father was a lawyer and his mother a businesswoman. They were both accomplished in their professions. They were both top in their high school classes and did extremely well on their college entrance exams. Pierre's dad went on to the University of Paris, Sorbonne, to study law. Pierre's mom went to the esteemed business school, ESSEC. There are debates as to whether this is the number one business school at the undergraduate level or if it's ranked number two in the way some Americans like to debate whether Harvard Law School or Yale's Law School is number one. Since high school, they knew exactly what they wanted to do. They worked hard in their undergraduate years and smoothly transitioned from their academic programs to professional life. Pierre's dad started to work for an American law firm in Paris and made an American lawyer's salary, which was higher than what typical French law firm paid experienced lawyers. Pierre's dad also worked American lawyer hours and that was actually his incentive for quitting after working only three years. He saved up quite a lot of money during that period since he had no debt from his law education. Pierre pointed out that French universities are practically free with only nominal registration fees. After quitting his job at the American law firm, Pierre's dad started working for a French law firm and rose all the way to the top.

Pierre's mom had to pay for her education at ESSEC because it is a private, specialized institution of higher learning unlike France's universities, which are all public and government owned and sponsored. But since Pierre's mom was from a well-to-do family in Paris, she also did not have any debt coming out with her business degree. Pierre's mom started to work first for an American company doing a lot of business in France. One of Pierre's mom's hobbies was reading, speaking, and writing English, so she studied quite a bit of English while she was getting her business education. Because English became more and more important in the business world of Paris, her good skills in English became a particular asset. She took advantage of stock options that was a part of an incentive program and saw the price of her stocks double, triple, and grow at an exponential rate as her American company expanded throughout Europe and also started businesses in Asia. Seeing opportunities in Asia through her company's efforts, Pierre's mom retired early from her company, having fulfilled her twenty minimum years to receive a pension, and she started a business of her own. Although her new company was a competitor in the Asian market with the American company she left behind, she was getting a large pension from her former company, so that the new business risk was not really a risk at all. She managed to succeed in her endeavor, and now she has one of the most important French companies that do import and export with Asian countries.

Financially, Pierre's family is better than well off. In fact, Pierre's family home is right in an exclusive part of Paris. Despite the high cost of property in Paris, they have a big garden where you could even hold a small wedding. The house is two stories high and is five bedrooms. It sounds quite modest, but when one realizes that this centrally located house has one large room to entertain guests, a big dining room with a dinner table for twelve guests and a spacious kitchen with its own dining room table and other common areas, one can begin to appreciate the extravagance of such a home.

Pierre's father and mother provided a fairly sheltered life for Pierre. And Pierre had a non-rebellious childhood. Pierre did his school work faithfully and spent most time at home with his family. Pierre did have friends, but mostly they met at his home or their homes. They were not so different from Pierre in the way that their parents provided shelteredness. Pierre's friends were quite brilliant and will most likely become what their parents are and perhaps even attain what Pierre's parents have achieved. Pierre was quite intelligent as well, but his interests did not lie in success, at least in the way his parents defined it. Pierre was not interested in making a lot of money or gaining social standing or making waves in whatever he decided to do. Pierre told me one time that his greatest goal in life was to find happiness.

I asked Pierre what would make him happy, and his answer was that he was still searching. The topic of happiness actually became an often discussed theme in our conversations. I know one thing that made him happy. Pierre loved rock music and even subscribed to several magazines on this genre when he was in France. Now that he was in Israel, his parents were sending him a bunch of rock magazines every month, and Pierre was quite eager for this mail. Pierre's parents supported Pierre beyond the call of duty. Despite all the properness of his parents, Pierre's parents allowed Pierre to have a drum set in the basement. There were rules surrounding when he could and when he could not practice and play. Pierre never broke the rules, but he did maximize the practice time that was allowed under his parents' roof.

There were rules not only about when he could play his drums or not, but there were also rules about everything else. Pierre's parents really wanted him to make waves in the world more than they did. Their philosophy was that politeness was the first step to getting anywhere. With this philosophy, which they often reiterated to Pierre, they set up boundaries all over Pierre's life. I don't think Pierre resented his parents for his constricted life. Pierre often spoke of his parents in the fondest of terms and was quite happy to share his positive experiences as a child and youth. On the other hand, Pierre might chime in with a bunch of American youths in saying that now that kind of life was not for him. It was, in fact, a monumental turning point in his life to be in Jerusalem. It was certainly the first time that Pierre lived away from home for a protracted time -- away from his parents' politeness rule system.

It wasn't the system *per se* that Pierre objected; otherwise, he would not act according to his upbringing. He was certainly polite, and his parents would be proud of the way he acted. However, Pierre was not happy with the strings that were attached to the Polite System, such as expectations for success along the lines that his parents defined them. Pierre wanted to be happy, and although he might not know what that exactly meant, he knew exactly what that was not. Happiness for Pierre certainly was not attached to material or worldly success. The question, of course, remained as to what would make Pierre happy. As his friend, I was determined that I would help him find his answers. This dinner that we were throwing for Orit and Orli certainly could be a piece of the puzzle and its solution.

After Orit and Pierre exchanged pleasantries, Orit introduced me and Pierre to Orli, her roommate. Orli was about the same height with Orit and with the same beautifully tanned complexion. She was wearing a white shirt with a drawing of elephants on it and words underneath the picture. It read, Poach eggs, not elephants. She was also wearing blue jeans. She had long flowing hair, which was black in color. Orli had beautiful brown eyes and a gentle, soft smile. She seemed a little bit shy at first. It might be that she found herself in an awkward situation of being introduced to two strangers from other countries in a small corridor, albeit in a cozy apartment that required her being inside for a while to feel the full impact of its coziness. Pierre was polite and even gracious in his extension of plea-santries, and this actually seemed to put Orli at a greater ease. I said my pleasantries, not as polished as Pierre's but in a typically gre-garious and friendly manner that I am used to and feel comfortable with for myself.

Orit handed me a bottle of wine. It was a semi-dry red wine. I told her that she didn't have to do that. Soon after, though, I wanted to show her that I appreciated it, so I said that we would share her wonderful gift all together and have it with the meal. I invited our guests to sit down by our banquet table. Pierre and I had pulled the table away from the wall shortly before Orit and Orli arrived, so there were four open sides now and four chairs for all of us. Orit sat by the long side facing the entrance door. Orli sat on the shorter side of the table with her back towards the door to our room and facing the kitchen sink. Pierre sat down on the other long side of the table with his back almost against the entrance door and facing Orit. I had wanted to sit facing Orit, but I realized that it was better to have her sit where she was. Although I would not be facing Orit directly, I realized that she would be closer to me physically than sitting way across the table at the opposite side. Although the table wasn't that big, closer distance was a good thing. There were more opportunities for eye contact, and physical proximity was certainly a good thing in making a personal connection, especially in conversation.

Pierre, Orit, and Orli were sitting. I wanted to give Pierre the opportunity to get to know Orit and Orli, so I tried to jump start the conversation with a statement to the effect -- Pierre is from France and you should hear all the interesting things that I have heard about the food culture in France. Pierre, you should tell Orit and Orli about that restaurant you love. Pierre looked at me giving me a nod with his eyes, turned to look at Orit and Orli, and then started to talk to them about his favorite restaurant. I was glad that Pierre was connecting with our guests. I wanted him to do so without any distractions, so I took a step or two towards the sink area and proceeded to open the bottle of wine.

It wasn't the easiest thing to do, since I was not so experienced in opening wine bottles, especially with the simplest of wine opening instruments. While opening the wine bottle, I did toss a couple of glances over to the direction of the table and was happy to see that Orit and Orli were absorbed in Pierre's detailed description of his favorite dishes at the restaurant. Pierre had a gift for describing his favorite food with a passion, and in a way that captured the curiosity and culinary desires of the listeners. I thought to myself that this was going really well. Pierre's story was like a verbal appetizer. Orit and Orli's appetites were surely being whetted with every passing second and with every enthusiastic adjective that described Pierre's favorite food. I finally got the bottle opened. Acknowledging the slight noise that this made, Pierre chimed in his pause in the narrative. Orit and Orli looked in the direction of the sound and were met by my smiling face. I told them, now, we were ready to start the meal.

The table was already set. This, we did before we moved the table away from the wall. Of course, in hindsight, we should have moved the table first and, then put the utensils and dishes on it, but we were not used to having guests at the dinner table. Having three open sides sufficed for all four of us in the apartment. Besides, our other two flatmates did not often eat dinner at home and certainly not during the regular dinner time that Pierre and I were getting used to. I was used to eating dinner around five or six, and Pierre was used to having dinner around seven or eight. We compromised and had dinner around six thirty. Our other flatmates, when they did have dinner in the apartment, ate around nine or ten in the evening. So, you could see that three open sides of the table were more than sufficient for Pierre and me. In fact, this time was the first time that we ever pulled the table out for the sake of dining. Even with all the utensils on the table, the table was not so hard to move. The floor was smooth, so the table slid nicely. We were not moving the table any great distance so the utensils and dishes, by and large, stayed in their respective places. All we had to do was to adjust them to look nice and neat.

Even now, I feel pride in the way the set table looked as I faced our guests with an open bottle of wine. There were glasses already set up on the table. I first took Orit's glass and poured her some wine. Orli's glass followed. I addressed Pierre's glass next and then mine last. With all of our glasses full, I thought about the best toast to offer. I thought, maybe it would be good to stick to a warm and friendly toast rather than any kind of toast with a romantic ring to it. So, I toasted our new found friendship. Everyone seemed to be happy with this toast. We all took only a sip.

Pierre and I were not experienced drinkers. I hardly drank when I was in the USA, and Pierre was probably the only Frenchman whom I met who didn't like wine and cheese. I got somewhat attached to Maccabee beer as Pierre and I began to socialize in the Israeli Bar scene. But we hardly ever drank more than a bottle or two in a given outing. And we weren't used to drinking a glass of wine before a meal. Even the sip we took was an effort of sorts. The semi-dry nature of the wine at least helped Pierre, since he was not too keen on dry wine. He told me that the only time he tried it in France, he almost threw up. Had Orit and Orli brought dry wine, you bet I would have found an excuse not to open it. But the fortunes seemed to be on our side that night, and all went smoothly so far.

I noticed that Orit and Orli only took one sip and put their glasses down. I was wondering if they were also not very much into wines. Before letting myself ponder these thoughts for too long and letting the pause and silence linger to the point where everyone would become uncomfortable, I interjected that it was time for the appetizer. I was sure to add that it was from mom's recipe all the way from the USA. I knew that this short addition was significant and would create the Oooh Effect. And that's exactly what happened. Granted, the expression was slightly different from that I was used to in the States. But the message that the exclamation of fondness carried was certainly equivalent.

I brought out the fried vegetables. Orit asked me what it was, and I was glad that she did. It showed her genuine interest and allowed my extensive explanation to seem natural. Volunteering details of one's own cooking could come off sounding pretentious and self-absorbed, so I was glad that Orit offered me the opportunity to elaborate at length about the food and its history in the most natural way. I quickly explained the ingredients. I thought that unless Orit and Orli were really into cooking, they would not be so interested in the recipe. I would only bore them. And I figured that if they were really interested in the recipe, either Orit or Orli or even both of them would ask questions about the precise nature of the recipe or even request that I write it down for them. What I thought would interest them was why this particular dish was important to me, personally. This would not only provide them with an interesting story, it would allow them to get to know me better as a person. Wasn't that one of the central purposes of Operation Food Know? For all of us to get to know each other better?

I told Orit and Orli that the dish was important to me because I grew up with it. Ever since I was a child, mom used to make this particular appetizer dish during important holidays and family gatherings. I added that as a child, I would often look forward to holidays and family gatherings at least partly because I would have the opportunity to taste this dish. I didn't, however, tell Orit, Orli, and

Pierre that there was somewhat of a disappointment after making the dish. I realized how simple the dish was to make. I almost felt foolish as I told them that I used to wait weeks and even months for this dish. I even asked myself as I was recounting the story to them why I was such an idiot and didn't learn to make this dish until now. I could probably have made this in junior high school. I was still trying to recover from these thoughts that ran through my mind as I was serving my dish. I tried to push them out of my mind because I wanted to concentrate on making Operation Food Know a success. I didn't want to be distracted.

But, perhaps, that was a mistake. Maybe I should have allowed my thoughts to wander and deal with the reality that dawned on me. But as it happened, I didn't, and as I verbalized how much I used to look forward to this dish, a rush of emotions flowed into me. It felt similar to finding out that there was no Santa Claus. Actually, it felt worse, since at least with the idea of Santa Claus, seeing Santa Claus's at shopping areas and at the church and practically everywhere gave me a hint even as a youngest child that, perhaps, there was no Santa Claus, or at least not one Santa Claus. But with the dish, it was different. It was quite personal and I developed a form of religious expectation that bordered on ritual.

I looked forward to the dish in my own way which resembled the way my grandma looked forward to the Second Coming of the Messiah. I had faith that I would be fully satiated by this dish and even believed that it helped to usher in the holiday, a day separated from normal, regular days, with its specialness. I had thought that making this dish for that day's dinner would have the same effect, at least symbolically. I was ushering in, perhaps, a new age for the Pierre-Samuel apartment. We were engaging in a cultural and international experience that might have momentous consequences. From what I could gather, no other foreigner in Jerusalem was engaging in a cross cultural project of our magnitude to bridge friendships/relationships in such a direct, straightforward fashion. Our success could pave the way for others like us who would be interested in making inroads into the Israeli culture. We could be the cultural trailblazers in Israel.

All these presupposed pictures of grandeur that this dish was to dignify came to naught in my realization that the dish was quite simple to make. The magic attached to the dish seemed to have evaporated. It was like finding out a treasured secret of a most awesome magic trick. I felt it in the most personal way. I tried to stop the rush of emotions that were filling inside me, but I couldn't. Becoming almost speechless, I quickly closed my narrative by saying that it's my favorite dish and I'm glad to be sharing it with them. I must have said the right thing. Orit gazed up at me from her seat with warm eyes and even gave me a wink. I smiled back. Then, I proceeded to take the fried vegetables from the bowl and began to distribute them to Orit, Orli, and Pierre. When we all had some on our plates, we began almost simultaneously to take a bite into the fried vegetables.

I don't know why, but I found myself a little nervous, almost vulnerable. That was precisely it. I felt vulnerable. I felt like I had something personally invested in their verdict on the sanctified appetizer. In the small fraction of time when they were all taking their bite, my thoughts raced. A negative judgment on the food could be a negative judgment on me, personally. After all, I've spent a good few minutes accounting how significant the food was for me and why I looked forward to it and to the special occasions in which I would be able to taste it. It was bad enough to realize that day that the dish was quite easy to make and that the mystic aura surrounding the dish had been stripped away. I could not imagine what kind of emotional effect their rejection would have on me.

As I finished my own bite and tasted the fried vegetables, I realized that it was actually quite tasty and approximated what I was used to at home. I remembered why I waited for this dish and for the family gathering events when I would be able to have this dish. I knew even before anyone spoke up, that this dish was a success. Even if none of them liked it, I knew that I had successfully recreated the mystic past in this very own room, certainly in terms of taste. This dinner table was now hallowed ground. One of my deepest experiences spanning many years of my childhood, youth, and even adulthood has dignified this dinner in a way that this dinner could no longer be a failure whatever happened in the course of the meal.

As I looked around, I realized that I have found three converts to my experience. I could read culinary pleasure on their faces. Even sounds of culinary ecstasy reached their high pitch. It was a natural sound of pleasure, so even before they spoke, I knew that I would be returned three resounding approvals. Praises came one after another. Pierre added the cherry on the top of the ice cream sunday, of course, figuratively speaking. He said that he could fully understand why I would await the holidays. Had he tasted this dish in his childhood, he would too have eagerly looked forward to special gatherings as I did. I knew that Pierre was quite polite, but I also knew that food was one true sacred thing for him.

Pierre would have found a polite thing to say without compromising his zealousness for food, had he found my food less than the judgment he was pronouncing before this culinary court. He would not have compromised what was so sacred to him. So, I felt doubly touched by his proffered comments. Orit added that she wanted the recipe after the dinner, so that she could share it with her family. Orli chimed in that she also wanted to share the dish with her family.

Pierre and I were quite excited by this response. I was excited because they thought it was good enough that they would make the effort to share it with their families. Pierre told me afterwards that he shared my excitement at their not mentioning sharing the dish with their boyfriends. I thought that a serious boyfriend would come before the family if they had boyfriends, since they were roommates and lived away from home. If they had boyfriends, it would be easier for them to share the dish first with their boyfriends who would certainly visit them on a regular basis. But the fact that they both mentioned sharing the dish with their families and did not mention their boyfriends indicated to me (and I was later to find out from Pierre that it was the case with him as well) that they did not have boyfriends. There was, of course, the possibility that they had boyfriends but simply forgot to mention them. Pierre added at the post-dinner wrap up session that if this were the case, then it was a good thing from our point of view, since they were forgetting their boyfriends in our presence. This would, according to Pierre, indicate one or both of two things. One, they were not in a serious relationship to feel the need to mention their boyfriends or even remember them when thinking about sharing great food. Two, even if they were in what might be termed as a relationship with someone, they felt an implicit need or even subconscious initiative not to mention them to us, possibly keeping options open for us in the relationship department.

I expressed my reservation in the case of the second situation. I knew that the Israelis have a saying that A Boyfriend Is Not A Wall. But it seemed somehow wrong to take a woman from her boyfriend. Kind of like theft. I remembered a discussion that I had with a female friend about this topic. I asked as a theoretical case what she thought about a guy who likes a girl and she reciprocates but she is in a relationship with another guy. My friend told me that she thought that love was most important and if the two loved each other, then, that would excuse their basically screwing over the other guy. I thought there was implicit unfairness to this and told her this. In response, she reiterated the familiar saying,

All's Fair in Love and War. Platitudes. Is that their only purpose? To provide an answer and defense against difficult situations?

I said to my friend that it seemed wrong to take a woman away from her boyfriend. She had a pretty good reply to this statement. She stated that the whole concept of taking a woman away from her man diminishes the woman's initiative in the relationship. Women are thinking individuals capable of making their own decisions, so if a woman leaves her boyfriend for another man, then, it is on her own initiative and no one has stolen her from someone else. I don't know if she realizes this, but her statement not only gives women initiative and what can be loosely termed as empowerment, but it also gives them res-ponsibility and the guilt. In the previous thinking that men stole women from their existing boyfriends, the new boyfriends were wholly responsible and the ex-boyfriends had in more than a few occasions showed the extent of their guilt with fists to their faces. The idea was that the new guy did not play fairly and broke one of the unspoken male rules.

By saying that women left on their own initiative, it gave women partnership in guilt for breaking the heart of their ex-boyfriends. Perhaps, when Foucault said that when one gains certain power, one also loses certain privileges, he was speaking truth. I shared this conversation that I had with my female friend with Pierre in the post dinner discussion in quite some detail. Pierre did not like Foucault very much despite the fact that Foucault was his countryman. Pierre, however, said that he had to agree with Foucault in his idea of power, at least in this case. Then, our post dinner conversation took on a highly philosophical tone and we ended up staying up until three AM in the morning engaging in a highly philosophical conversation without any particular direction. I remember one professor saying that best ideas are born through digression. Perhaps, during one of these conversations, I will come up with an idea that will make a significant positive changes for humanity. Who knows?

I was quite excited that Orit and Orli wanted my recipe, and I did not hide my excitement at their request. I was going to be sure to give them the recipes after dinner. Now, I announced, will be the main course that Pierre had specially prepared for this wonderful occasion. I asked Pierre to explain his dish. I wanted to give Pierre as much time as possible to speak and to show Orit and Orli what a wonderful and interesting person he was. I felt a little nudge here and there were necessary because I noticed that he tended to be more taciturn around people with whom he was not very familiar. Whenever we had conversations together in the apartment, Pierre never failed to express his views, and it was actually quite interesting to hear him talk. I wanted Orit and Orli to see that, so I gave him a little nudge to talk about the dish that he labored over for their benefit. I knew that food was one topic that Pierre would not have difficulty enthusing over. I just had to open the door for him, and I did so consciously knowing of positive results that were to come.

As expected, Pierre's enthusiasm over his honey glazed chicken rose with every passing word. His excitement was actually quite contagious. Pierre went into every detail about his master creation, step by step, leaving no details out. Yet, Orit and Orli seemed spellbound. I was forming several theories to explain this phenomena. Despite the fact that even contagious enthusiasm wears off after a while, Pierre was able to capture their attention, possibly, because everyone loves English spoken with a French accent. Perhaps, not everybody, but almost every female person that I had a chance to consult about this question confirmed that French accent is quite smoothly melodious and certainly pleasant to listen to. Another possible reason was that women found him physically attractive in an exceptional way. Who else in the whole land of Israel or the United States for that matter had several women in different places and times taking a picture of him and letting him know that they were doing so because they found him physically attractive? It might happen to some famous models, but Pierre was an unknown. I would not have been surprised if Orit and Orli were, at least, partly under the same spell.

Third possible reason is that they just loved cooking and cuisine and topics pertaining to them were of immense interest to them. This would certainly be confirmed by their wanting the recipe for my appetizer. I have been invited to dinners before and tasted some amazing food but never before did I ask for a written recipe. Although I liked cooking from time to time and enjoyed consuming good food, I was far from being a recipe junkie or being in any explicit or implied fan club for cooking. But if I tasted a home cooked meal that was simply amazing, I might be compelled to ask for the recipe. Who knows? In regards to this situation with Pierre, my bet was that there was a combination of these factors that led to their visibly enchanted interest in Pierre's account. Although I had expected Orit and Orli to find Pierre interesting as he expounded on the topic of his passion, I had no idea that he would have this strong effect on them. I was quite happy to see this as I noticed that Pierre was overflowing with smiles.

Spurred on by their encouraging gaze, Pierre continued to describe the significance of the dish for him.

I learned something new from the continued narrative. Pierre told Orit, Orli, and me that the recipe was passed onto his mom from her mom. Pierre's mom started to use it only occasionally during Friday night meals, so for Pierre, the honey glazed chicken dish almost encapsulated his memories of Shabbat meals in France. Pierre's mother was not religious and neither was Pierre's father, but Pierre said that they were intricately concerned about their Jewish identity, so they encouraged Jewish cultural practices, which often had deeper religious significance for Jews who are more observant of religious practices. This was the case with the Friday night meals that Pierre's family had. They were referred to as Shabbat meals, and even prayers were read at the beginning of the meal. Male members of the household were required to wear a kippah, also referred to as yamulkah, during the prayer ceremonies, although they were allowed to take them off afterwards. The father actually led the way by taking his off right after the prayers and some traditional rites that were incorporated into the beginning of the meal.

Pierre, therefore, thought that his mom had a greater hand in trying to preserve some of the forms of the Friday Shabbat meal. Pierre once commented to me that if it weren't for his mom, the Friday evening meal would be like any other meal. Pierre shared, now, with all of us that he felt that his mom consciously made the honey glazed chicken a symbol of the Shabbat meal. Pierre thought that she inherited this concept from within the Jewish tradition. There are such dishes as latckis, a potato dish, and also jelly doughnuts which are seen as traditionally belonging to Hanukkah. These dishes bind the children to the holiday in a collective memory as a community, according to Pierre.

Pierre shared that his mother trying to create a special symbolism with her honey glazed chicken was not so different in concept to the symbolism of food found during the Passover Seder meal. It is a meal to remember God's faithfulness as found in the book of Exodus, where he delivered the Israelites from slavery in Egypt, according to Pierre. In this celebratory meal, I was told, there are guidelines as to when to consume certain foods and how to consume them as well. At one point, a child is supposed to ask his father, How is this night different from any other night? Food symbolism and religious ritual functioned in a didactic way to foster community and reiterate collective religious memory. Pierre felt that his mom was highly conscientious of Jewish history and experience and wanted to create identity symbols for her children, although she was agnostic and did not believe in God or the Bible. Pierre shared that he had high respect for his mom for the effort she exerted to provide a stable home for them and to foster a clear sense of identity.

But later on at the post-dinner conversation, Pierre shared with me his doubts as to how significant these symbols were. Pierre raised a question which he said would be taboo in his household. What good are religious symbols when one doesn't believe? Perhaps, Pierre addressed this question not really to me but rather to himself. You see, at the dinner, after Pierre gave his account of the significance of his food and even shared his personal family experience with Jewish religious symbolism and practice, Orit responded by saying that she had never had a Shabbat meal with prayers in her life. Orit shared that her parents were secular Jews who actually did not like religious Jews that much. Orit cared about the unity of the Israeli people, so even though she was secular, she tried to encourage her parents not to be so harsh on religious Jews. But her parents were adamant in their dislike of religious Jews. Orit shared that she often heard her parents say that their hard earned wages and their taxes were going to feed yeshiva students who did nothing but study the Torah, Jewish religious texts, while receiving money from the Israeli government for this.

Orit almost winced as she repeated what her father called religious Jews in Israel. He referred to them as parasites, and this was, in fact, his nickname for them. Orit said that she got so tired of hearing her father call religious people parasites that she dropped her efforts to convince her father to be more accepting of religious Jews in Israel. Orit just avoided the whole topic with her dad. Orit mentioned that her mother often chimed in support of her father. Her mother would often add that God was not going to save Israel but the Israeli Army will. Orit's mother had served in the Israeli Army and was proud of that. Orit's mother was resentful of the fact that none of the religious women or men, for that matter, served in the army, citing religious reasons. Orit's mom complained to Orit on numerous occasions that religious Jews in Israel took their money and the benefits of Israeli government hand-outs but neither did any work nor participate in defending the country.

Orit's mom further told Orit that there were even some in the religious Jewish community in Israel that were opposed to the State of Israel's existence because they believed that only the Messiah was to usher in Israel's statehood. The present government of Israel was referred to by some in religious groups as an abomination to God. Orit confessed that although she did not like it when her parents were so critical of the religious population in Israel, she did share some resentment against religious Jews in Israel. She thought that they should participate more in Israeli life, for instance, by serving in the army.

Pierre sat surprised by what Orit was sharing, and, to top it off, Orit directly looked at Pierre and said that she thought when one is not religious, one should not pretend to be religious. Trying to use religious identity to foster Jewish identity, according to Orit, was ethically dishonest. I felt uncomfortable about the way the conversation was going. However, it was obvious that this topic was an important one for Orit. She decided to be frank about her sentiments, and I recognized that this could be a good sign. She felt com-fortable enough to share with us about not only her personal thoughts but also her criticisms of her parents. But I was worried at that moment that Pierre might not be able to see the whole picture so accurately and might misinterpret Orit's comments as a personal attack. To diffuse the situation a little bit at least, I quickly jumped into the conversation that was becoming more bilateral between Pierre and Orit, with both of them looking directly at each other. I pronounced that the wonderful honey glazed chicken was now being served. It did certainly bring smiles to everyone's face. It took longer time with Pierre and Orit, but they came, actually quite quickly after the smile on Orli's face.

I was hoping that I could turn the conversation to another topic, but I was sure that I would not be able to when after the honey glazed chicken was served, Pierre and Orit were staring at each other. They were not looking at each other in a hostile way, but the desire, or perhaps the determination, to continue the discussion clearly showed on their faces. I thought that the best I could do under this circumstance was to de-personalize the conversation to generic levels. That'll keep the meal pleasant, according to my American sensibilities, and we might even learn some things in the process. So, I asked Orit what she thought was a good, general way to foster one's identity. Orit responded by saying that she had really not thought much about the question of fostering a conscious identity. She said that she only grew up knowing Jews in her neighborhood, and everyone knew that they were Jews. They did not need to justify to anybody that they were Jews, and no one asked them to.

Orli added that she knew what Orit meant. Perhaps, because they were Jews living in the Jewish State of Israel, their Jewish identity was affirmed by their merely living in the country. Orli forwarded that one did not need to try to preserve Jewish religious traditions in Israel to feel Jewish. There were no need to distinguish Jews from others in Israel because most towns were one hundred per cent Jewish. There were towns that were non-Jewish, but they were usually one hundred per cent non-Jewish. Often, Jews from Israeli towns did not come in regular contact with non-Jews in non-Jewish towns. So, conscious questioning about identity was often unnecessary. Orli added that she felt more Israeli than Jewish. Orli further said that she was like Orit and identified herself with the secular camp. She was proud to be an Israeli and felt secure in that identity. For Orli, Judaism as a religion did not matter so much. But Orli was quick to add that Jewish history and experience was important to her, and, these, she learned in her schooling all the way from kindergarten to high school, so she did not need to go out of her way to learn about it.

As if offering a conclusion to the conversation, Orli looked at Pierre, smiled at him, and then even reached out her right hand to touch his shoulder. I noticed that Pierre was not unhappy with this late development. Orli told Pierre that he should make aliyah and immigrate to Israel; then, he could be a part of this wonderful society where one didn't have to wrestle constantly with one's Jewish identity as if one were somehow separated from it and needed to capture it. He will be Jewish just by living in Israel. Pierre did not offer an answer but did politely smile back. I was able to see that a thought has taken hold in his mind.

I would not have been surprised if Pierre was already contemplating it at that point. Granted, Pierre did not mention his desire to immigrate to Israel, but I realized as time passed that Pierre's reflections on France and his experiences there took on a tone of speaking about the Old Country. His description of his experiences back in France almost came to take on a mythic distance and an ethereal presence. He would often interject at moments about how the wonderful French did such and such. He spoke of France and French culture in glowing terms as time passed. I knew that Pierre liked the fact that he had a French origin, but a change was clear in that his assessment of France gradually took on an uncritical tone as time passed. This was markedly different from our conversations during the first few days of being roommates. It's possible that nostalgia played a role in this regard.

But it wasn't the kind of nostalgia in which he wanted to go back to France. It was a nostalgia of the kind in which he was resigned to giving up his France to the area of his mythic past experience and memory. The only description of France that I found was a constant was Pierre's glowing description of French cuisine. This dinner might have been a turning point for Pierre in his contemplation of making aliyah. But Pierre never shared with me about this contemplation, and to my knowledge, he did not share it with anyone else. His parents often ended their conversation over the phone by saying that they were looking forward to having Pierre back in France after the end of a year's stay, Pierre told me. So, if he were going to immigrate, it was a decision that Pierre was going to make by himself.

All the serious discussion did not allow ample time for Pierre's marvelous creation to be praised, but it was obvious from four empty plates that the dish was a great success. Orli offered the first compliment for the dish. She actually said that it was the best chicken dish that she tasted in her life. Pierre was all smiles. I could see that Pierre, at last, put to the back of his mind the serious discussion that preceded the compliment. Orit was also earnest in praising Pierre's dish, and I added my seal of approval and adulation as well.

On that sweet note we entered the time for dessert. Pierre told me earlier that he was a little bit apprehensive about how his dessert would be received. I thought that Pierre's chocolate mousse turned out just right, but I could see that Pierre solicited the mental image of his mother's chocolate mousse as a standard to indict the dessert over which he had exerted much more effort than he had done over the honey glazed chicken. My effort with fried vegetables certainly paled in comparison to the effort Pierre put into making his honey glazed chicken. Granted, a part of the reason for Pierre's exertion was that we did not have an egg beater, so Pierre had to beat the white of the egg with a spoon. Maybe it was the part of me that held to the American dream that one who works hard should be rightly compensated or the part of me that was faithful in friendship to Pierre, or both, which caused me to believe that Pierre's dessert would be a great success. And in truth, I thought the chocolate mousse looked just beautiful. It certainly smelled great.

I knew about the insecurities that Pierre was feeling regarding his chocolate mousse, so I decided not to give him any deliberate forum to speak. There was a good chance that he might give a self-defeating speech about how he had hoped for a better chocolate mousse but ended up with a flatter chocolate mousse than the one he was used to seeing from his mom's creations. I looked over in Pierre's direction to see if he wanted to say something. If he did want to say something, I had no right not to give him the opportunity. Seeing that my assessment of the situation was an accurate one and when I noticed Pierre looking at me with a visible message not to give him the floor, I introduced the dessert to Orit and Orli as one of the gloriously chocolate desserts they will ever taste. I knew that the central ingredient was a gourmet chocolate. Even if Orit and Orli happened to be the two leading chocolate mousse experts in Israel, they could not help but to appreciate the chocolate contained in the dessert.

It was confirmed that Orit and Orli were both chocolate lovers. Their eyes became wide with pleasure when they saw the chocolate mousse, and I was sure that the glorious odor had no small part to play in encouraging Orit and Orli. There was enough for a modest serving for everyone. I have to encourage Pierre to make more next time, I thought as I served the portions. Perhaps, I was thinking from the perspective of my American ex-perience. We had drink sizes that could not be found anywhere else in the world. Even for McDonald's, not all McDonald's were created equal. What was a small or medium sized drink in an American McDonald's was equi-valent to a large or even super large size in McDonald's outside of the USA. Maybe it was my being used to generous portions that found the amount too much of a teaser. But I don't think so.   After about four spoon fulls, we found our plates quite empty of the delicious content.   It was obvious that Orit and Orli wanted more. Leave them wanting more. This may be one of Pierre's themes for tonight, I thought.

I couldn't believe that the dinner was already coming to a close. I offered coffee, wishing to prolong the wonderful event just a little bit longer. No one refused, so I started to boil some water. I borrowed my other flat-mate's electric water boiler for this purpose. I have gotten used to this electric water boiler by now, but when I first saw it, I did not know what to make of it. I had never seen anything like it in the United States.

This is the way the water boiler worked. There was a water container which opened at the top, so one could place water through it. After closing the lid, one inserted the plug, attached to the whole apparatus, to the wall electric outlet. Then, one had to press down the switch to start the boiling process. Within three minutes or so, there would be enough water boiled to serve more than four cups of coffee. I, first, found myself distrusting the water electric boiler when I had the chance to look inside the container. There was a metallic small pipe that was coiled around inside on the bottom of the electric boiler. It was obvious from just looking at it that electricity heated up this pipe which caused the water to boil. The problem in my mind was that the pipe had turned a whitish-green color. And there were bits and pieces of this color material at the bottom of the water whenever we boiled water.

Usually, there were enough water boiled that these small pieces did not get poured over into coffee and tea cups. But the matter was there at the bottom of the container. Who knows what's in that stuff? I asked my flatmate who owned the electric water boiler for his expert opinion regarding the matter. Since he had it for a few years, I figured he would be able to tell me the details that I needed to know. Surely enough, he told me that it was time for cleaning it. He added that there was a powdery material, which can be purchased from any grocery store or even the market place, that one inserted inside the container. With hot water or even boiling water inside, the powdery material would act like an acid agent and dissolve the whitish-green stuff stuck to the pipes, leaving only the original small pipe coil. I tried this and it worked fine. But this process was to be repeated once every month. This just became a reminder of my original question as to whether this devise was safe to use. I found every single friend that I had in Israel using this thing, so I figured it must either be safe, or we were all going to suffer together, if research showed that this device was harmful, after all. Eventually, I came to the conclusion that it was better not to give it any longer thought.

When the water boiled, I brought out the instant NesCafe jar and took a spoon full of coffee for each cup. It was relatively an easy process. I asked if any one of them wanted sugar. Only Pierre wanted sugar, so I added some sugar to Pierre's coffee. Everyone wanted some milk with their coffee, so I brought out the milk from the refrigerator. While I was working on making the coffee, I was happy to see that Orli was engaging Pierre in a conversation. Orli asked Pierre what he thought about Israel, so far. Pierre was generous with his praises and even provided some clear examples to support his praise. Orli seemed quite pleased by Pierre's response. I didn't want to interrupt this nice rapport that Pierre and Orli were having, but I also considered the fact that Orit might feel left out by their conversation. Pierre was slightly turned toward Orli and facing somewhat away from Orit. So, I quickly distributed coffee to everyone.

While sitting down, sipping coffee, I realized that some kind of closure conversation for the meal was needed. I noticed that Orit tended to be quite direct in her comments, so I turned to Orit and just asked her point blank what she thought of the dinner. Orit told me that she loved it. She added that she and Orli wanted to invite Pierre and me to dinner at their place the following week. Pierre and I knew, then, that Operation Food Know was a complete success.

Both Pierre and I started to thank Orit and Orli, simultaneously, and in a disorganized way. Orit and Orli seemed pleasantly taken aback by this show of enthusiasm, and they smiled. Orit and Orli asked me if they could help me and Pierre clean up. Of course, both of us profusely declined. The conversation was heading in the direction of goodbye. I, however, remembered that they wanted the recipe to fried vegetables. But I didn't want to break up this nice salutation and then make them wait until I wrote down the recipe on a piece of paper. So, I asked them if I should bring the recipe with me to the dinner. Orit and Orli said that this would make them very happy. So, on this very pleasant note we closed the wonderful dinner event at the Pierre-Samuel apartment. Even after Orit and Orli left, Pierre and I were quite happy and even expressed our surprise at how well the dinner had gone. Orit and Orli obviously enjoyed the food. And they were clearly comfortable enough to share some of their deep thoughts and personal experiences as well. Now, we even had the wonderful dinner to look forward to. At that moment, Pierre and

I did not know how things could get any better.

8

Project Pierre

It wasn't the most fun thing to look forward to cleaning up. Despite the fact that we were quite elated from the wonderful dinner that went before, we realized how tired we were with the success of the momentous dinner behind us. Just a few hours ago, we cleaned up the apartment after cooking and preparing for hours. Now, we were going to spend a sizable block of time washing dishes, cleaning up, and making the apartment as clean as it was before the meal. In fact, Pierre and I both knew that we needed to exert extra effort to making sure that the apartment was in tip top shape. We could not have our two flatmates thinking that it's a bad idea to have us throw dinner parties. If it were just Pierre and me in the apartment, I might even have proposed that we clean up in the morning since it was the weekend after all. Despite Pierre's properness and concern for neatness, I would not have been surprised if he agreed this time. But I guess it was a good thing for all of us involved that we were cleaning up right afterwards. Even though our two flat-mates might have been a motivating force behind our cleaning up, we knew that we would be happier in the morning because we would not have the mess to clean up. That way, we could start the new day and take it in whichever direction we wanted to. Besides, the cleaning-up stage provided a transitional stage from the sacred event of dinner festivities to the profane space of ordinary time.

The cleaning up actually turned out to be not so bad. I washed the dishes, and Pierre cleaned up the table and swept and mopped the floor. It must have taken no longer than thirty minutes. Pierre and I did not talk much while we were doing our respective duties. I, for one, was savoring in my mind the wonderful dinner and evening that we had. I was replaying in my mind my favorite parts of the dinner. Most of all, I was thinking about how beautiful Orit looked. I certainly learned a little bit more about her, today. I had to say that her direct style was not unattractive. Although I thought at the time that she could have been gentler with Pierre, I knew that Orit did not come out directly and strongly the way she did because she wanted to offend Pierre. It was just her style. Orit was a direct person. Wasn't this better after all? To know her real thoughts? She was being direct but that certainly did not detract from her being sweet and considerate. She was after all considerate to offer her positive assessment of the food and let us know how much she appreciated every dish as well as the whole meal fellowship. Pierre and I were assured that Orit's comments were honest and true since she was direct and unabashedly shared her opinions, even though they contradicted and even had the possibility to offend.

And how about Orli? I definitely remember her gazing with interest at Pierre. Pierre seemed to be enchanted by her. Of course, I had the possibility of definitively ascertaining Pierre's sentiment. So, as soon as I finished my duties, I resolved, I was going to ask Pierre about this. Pierre must have wanted some questions answered since he asked me if I wanted to drink another cup of coffee and reflect about the meal that we had. I eagerly agreed since I was excited about the evening and was interested in chatting with Pierre about it.

It was almost midnight, and we were drinking coffee. I knew that we weren't going to be going to bed any time soon. But I doubt we would have been able to fall asleep even if we had decided to turn in. We were physically worn out from the long day but rejuvenated by our experience and the immediate memory of the event. So, there we were, Pierre and I, sipping our coffee by the table, now pushed back against the wall in its original position. I sat where I sat during the meal, facing Pierre and the door through which Orit and Orli made their departure. Pierre looked comfortable in his dinner table seat.

Pierre started the conversation with a question. He asked what I thought about Orli.

I told Pierre that I thought she was beautiful and that she impressed me as a kindhearted person. Pierre inserted his agreement with nods while I was speaking and, then, jumped in with his praises of Orli's beauty. Pierre loved what she was wearing because it accentuated her beautiful body. Also, Orli had an angelic face. Pierre said that he could stare into Orli's eyes for hours. They were like black pearls. Encouraged by Pierre's vividly expressed regard for Orli, I asked a direct question regarding the precise nature of Pierre's sentiment for Orli. I surmised that Pierre liked Orli romantically from the way he praised her and eagerly asked about my opinions regarding her. But I wanted him to admit to himself out loud and profess to me, so that the point would be established and our conversation could build from there.

Pierre answered my question right away. He told me that it was like love at first sight. When he saw her for the first time by our doorway, he thought that his heart skipped a beat. And, then, his heart was beating louder and louder and faster and faster. Pierre said that he was afraid that we might be able to hear his heart beat. I was quite surprised by this revelation. I had an idea that Pierre was interested in her, but I didn't know that he was so deeply affected. I remembered our conversations from before about how one could tell what love is.

Pierre was convinced that passion must accompany love, and without it, love was not love. Furthermore, there had to be an element of automatic bodily reaction that was not contrived or forced, such as a faster heartbeat. Pierre shared that there were only few moments in his life that he experienced this. Once, it happened in a music store in Paris. Pierre was checking out his favorite music compact disks in the rock music section. As he was excitedly looking over the latest release of his favorite band, he caught a glimpse of a woman from the corner of his eyes. She had long brown hair and brown eyes. She had a light skin complexion which looked very smooth and silky. She was carrying a gentle and subtle smile. She was also in the rock music section looking through several compact disks. As soon as Pierre allowed his gaze to wander in her direction and saw the whole person before him, his heart skipped a beat, and he felt his heart pounding.

Pierre described that he really wanted to start a conversation, as she was only a few steps away from him. But whenever he tried to speak, he felt himself almost suffocating. He said that he had hard time even breathing because his heart was beating faster and faster. He didn't want to look so obvious and even strange looking at her, so he made sure that it looked like he was looking at the compact disk in front of him and contemplating about buying it. He didn't know whether he did a good job. But, maybe, he said, he should have been more focused on getting some kind of conversation started with her. Minutes passed, and she picked out the CD she wanted and then headed towards the cashier. Pierre contemplated chasing after her but thought that it would look strange, and he felt awkward about doing that, so he didn't. And he never saw her again. Paris is a big city.

Another time, Pierre was in the Paris metro when a similar thing happened. Once, Pierre stepped into a subway train car and immediately noticed a beautiful blonde woman sitting down diagonally across from the train door through which he entered. She was there with a friend of hers with whom she was sharing a vivid conversation. Pierre said that he could tell from just looking at her talk, that she was full of life. And this animation of hers accentuated her beauty. Her blonde hair flow-ed and moved graciously as she talked with her friend and Pierre saw the brightness and beauty of her blue eyes. This time, too, Pierre felt his heart beat pounding within his chest. He wanted so much to talk with her. But again, when he tried to say something from his seat which was almost directly across from where she was, he could not get a word out. And the next stop, she and her friend got off. In the hope that this subway train ride was a regular one on her part, Pierre even took the train at the same time for a couple of weeks. But, no, Pierre was not to see her again.

Pierre commented, after recounting the two events in his life, that he might have let the love of his life get away. Pierre said that at least he was happy to have experienced his heart racing like that at the sight of those two women, even though he wasn't able to do much more than look at them and appreciate them. He asked me if it was possible that some people don't even have that experience. Pierre asked this question and explained his reasons for asking the question. Practically contradicting himself, Pierre said that, maybe, it would have been better for him not to have had those two experiences because he would not have known the feeling of knowing that there were these two women who might be his soul mate, and he didn't do anything about it. He felt like he was cursed not to find happiness because it was not once but twice that he found himself totally incapable of action when he faced a woman who moved him in such a special way. At least, if he had not seen them, then, he could have said to himself that if he ever saw his soul mate, he would pursue her with all his might. Now, with the experience of these two women, he could not honestly say that to himself, let alone to others.

I disagreed with him during that conversation, of course being sensitive to his experiences. I thought that it was important to experience feeling something for someone in such a special manner, even if one might not find total fruition to one's feelings. I shared that it would be a total shame if one went his whole life, never knowing that there was a possible soul mate out there. It was possible for a person to be studying in a classroom and his possible soul mate to walk by in the hallway in front of the classroom. They would be only few feet away from each other but never meet. And they might die not knowing of each other's existence and the possibility of fulfilling the soul-mateship that they could have formed and enjoyed rest of their life. It was possible for the man to find some one and even fall in love and get married, and the same could happen to the woman. But they might not experience the extent of happiness that their being together as soul mates might have created. At least, Pierre knew that there were two women who moved him like no other did, and there's always a chance that he could run into them in the future.

I remembered this conversation that Pierre and I had shared. I wondered if Pierre remembered it or not. In light of this conversation, I knew that Pierre was now hopelessly in love. But what set this case apart from the other two is that, somehow, he felt comfortable enough to share a part of himself with Orli, whereas he wasn't able to do so with the two women in Paris. Orli now knew something about Pierre, and I was willing to bet that Orli went off that day with a very favorable impression of Pierre. What's more, Orit and Orli invited us to dinner for the following week. Pierre will have a greater opportunity to share himself with Orli. And the relationship that four of us were beginning to share was comfortable enough that I was willing to bet that there was a high likelihood of a relationship between Orli and Pierre. Furthermore, I thought that Orli seemed attracted to Pierre. If this was true, then the relationship between Orli and Pierre was basically a matter of time. I decided to share my conclusion with Pierre. I told him that I thought Orli was interested in him as well and that I thought it was very possible that he and Orli could end up becoming an item. It certainly must have been the right response he was looking for his implicit and implied question running through the conversation. Pierre told me that this would simply be wonderful.

Pierre asked me how he could transition from what was now a developing friendship between four people to a possible relationship for himself and Orli. I told Pierre that it might be a good idea to give that some thought before the actual dinner date the following week. Pierre started to express his doubts. What if Orli only likes him as a friend? He didn't want to do anything to jeopardize the friendship that was forming. On the other hand, he really liked Orli and wanted her to be more than a friend. Although our developing friendship with Orit and Orli was not ironclad or categorized as a friendship without the possibility of romance, Pierre hit on a perennial question. How does one transition from a friendship to a romantic relationship?

Friendship between a man and a woman seems to be a difficult thing, especially when one of the two wants more than merely platonic friendship, and the other might not think the same. I have seen awkwardness even in cases in which a male friend asks a female friend out on what would resemble a date. There's no clear definition that it's a date. Since the relationship started as a friendship, the woman may think that they were out doing something just as friends. And it's awkward for the guy to say unequivocally to her that they were going to be out on a date with a possible romantic potential. There seems to be an unspoken but universal law against saying something like that. With such a gray zone, it's harder to make the move toward romantic fulfillment. Since there's a friendship already in place, there's a certain amount of closeness and physical rapport. One would think that it's easier to make a romantic gesture on this basis, but that's not always the case. If a man were out with a woman who is not really his friend, then any gesture or sign of affection or endearment could be more confidently interpreted as a sign that she might be interested in something romantic. But when a man and a woman are friends, the same sign might be merely a form of friendly affection. So, a woman touching a man frequently can be seen as being just friendly in the case of friends. Even in the case of dating, this might be the case -- she might just be a very friendly person -- but there is a greater possibility that she is extending a romantic hint.

This struggle is not merely confined to the male sex. I remember having coffee with a friend, in the loose sense of the term, back in the US, and she said that she likes her dates to be clearly dates. She said that she liked being asked out on a date, and she wanted to know that it was clearly a date and not just friends getting together. I found this interesting because this pointed to her desire not to be confused as to the nature of the outing. She said that she was traditional in holding to this position. I wondered if it comes down to this.

Making a clear distinction between going out with someone on a date and hanging out with a friend of an opposite sex was a traditional thing and must be made consciously. She also added that she didn't believe in a crossover from being friends with a man to having a romantic relationship with him.

Although I remembered my conversation with her, I decided not to share this conversation with Pierre. It certainly was not going to help the current situation and would only discourage Pierre. Furthermore, her position might be just that -- her position. There may be many who believe that transitioning from friendship to romance was not only possible but even desirable. Orli may hold to that position. Besides, Pierre and my relationship to Orit and Orli was somewhat unique. We were not friends in any real sense of that term. I met Orit and invited her and her roommate to have dinner with me and Pierre in our apartment. It could be seen as a friendly gesture, but it could also be seen as a gesture filled with possible romantic content. What went on at the dinner could even be described as a double date, and it would not have been totally inaccurate to do so. What I wanted to do most at the post dinner wrap up conversation with Pierre was to be a supportive friend, showing him possibilities rather than the possible negative hurdles. I thought honestly that there was a real possibility that Pierre and Orli could end up together in a meaningful relationship. Pierre was obviously very interested in Orli. And from the look of Orli and her interaction with Pierre, I would say that she shared Pierre's sentiment. But I did recognized the importance of not letting Pierre's relationship with Orli resigning to friendship by lack of action on his part. I have certainly seen this happen, not with Pierre but with other friends.

I remember one case in which I introduced a male friend of mine to a female friend of mine. The first time, we all went out together. He with me and she with her friend. Knowing both of them, I knew that they would not have been comfortable with a blind date. We found the perfect setting in a water park. There were many things to do together which were fun, so that my two friends could get to know each other in a comfortable setting. There was, of course, certain amount of pressure for my friends, who knew that they were being set up. But the environment certainly mitigated the pressure. They were able to talk naturally while standing in line or walking from a water ride to water ride. They both loved water and anything relating to water sports, so the water park was the perfect setting. I knew that it wasn't necessarily the case with all of my friends. Some might feel uncomfortable being in a swim suit at the first meeting. Their reservations, of course, should be respected as well. People are different and have different preferences as well as reservations. At least with these two friends, their reservations did not include being in swim wear on the first contrived meeting.

I found out that day that their favorite ride was the wild water rafting ride. It turned out that the ride was a favorite of quite a number of other people as well. We waited in the line for quite some time. All of us were holding a big soda in one of our hands. The day was a perfect day for the beach. Blue skies with hardly any clouds. The temperature must have been easily over ninety degrees Fahrenheit. If it weren't for the intermittent cool water rides and soda iced up to the top, we might have been miserable waiting in lines. But we were all in high spirits, and the park, which was a first time experience for all of us, was turning out to be quite a wonderful experience. This positive mood definitely contributed to the free flow of conversation while we waited in the long line for the wild water rafting ride.

I was talking with my female friend's friend, so that left my two friends, whom I introduced to each other, for a conversation together. They talked and talked, and I tried not to eavesdrop on their conversation. It was a little difficult since we were standing right next to each other all together in the line. One thing I was hoping for was that they would start personalizing their conversation. However, the topic seemed to linger around the issue of water sports. Even this conversation could have been personalized to include exciting or even embarrassing moments in the past. Something to let each other know that they were making a personal connection was badly needed. A message had to be sent that he was interested in her in a personal way and would be happy to bring her into his confidence. Of course, it could go in the other direction as well. But some kind of personal connection had to happen, and it wasn't happening.

I know that I should have been attentive with the person that I was speaking with, but I felt I had so much invested in seeing them get together. After all, they were perfect for each other. I was sure that they would be happy together. I wanted so badly for them to get together that I drank my soda filled with ice too quickly, and I had one of those brain freeze moments. I felt my whole head go numb and even felt that I needed to close my eyes for a moment. It was like my head suddenly filled with cold soda, making it dysfunctional. My conversation partner asked me if I was okay. It must have been the first time I gave her my full attention. I told her that I was okay, and I thanked her for her concern. When my head cleared, I heard them, my two friends, talking about water sports in the most objective and theoretical terms.

Soon, we were in front of the line, ready to take the wild water rafting ride of a life time, or at least the most wet wild water rafting ride. They had gratuitous water falls at various points of the ride route where some if not all of the riders were bound to get completely wet. In some sense, though, this ride was not as fun here in the water park as in a general amusement park. There, the riders are fully clothed, so the surprise of who might be the most wet at the end of the ride provides a form of an amusing race and entertainment of sorts.

It was actually a form of gambling. Everyone was gambling on himself that he would not get wet. And the gambling involved an element of the ridiculous and social deviation in the normative social context that tickled the proper bone, if there is such a thing. There was fun in getting wet with one's clothes on. It bordered on the taboo. In a normal everyday activity, a person who gets wet is expected to get changed, right away. It would embarrass most people to walk around with wet clothing, especially if the water spots were accentuated in certain parts of one's clothing. But when one is at an amusement park, it is different. One could be fully clothed and even fully wet, and it could look like the most natural thing in the world. Some people might look, but all know that the wet person just came out of a water ride. No one would think of the person as violating some kind of social protocol or acting in an anti-social or deviant way in the context of an amusement park.

This, of course, raises the question of the context in human behavior. Why is it that we are so context bound? One appearance that is totally acceptable in one context is totally unacceptable in another setting. Walking around with wet clothes in a regular city street will raise eyebrows and some might even think that the person was not quite all right in his head. But it was perfectly fine in an amusement park. How about walking around in a swim suit?

By the way, what's really the difference between a bikini and wearing a bra and panties? Anyway, it's totally acceptable to walk around in one's glorified and more expensive version of the bra and panties in the beach area. But if one walked around in such a garb in the city or in one's neighborhood, people will raise eye brows and even think you were not all right in the head. Of course, some men in the neighborhood might be very excited by the development, but that's another issue.

The point certainly is there -- human beings value contexts and often see things through the lens of the context in which we find ourselves. And this not merely confined to the way people dress either. Behavior, often, is judged based on context. Most people have heard of the phrase, When in Rome, Do as the Romans Do. This encapsulates the context bound nature of human experience and culture. Implicit in the idea is the understanding that it is wise to do what would be normal for the Romans when one is in Rome because if one does not act according to the practices of the region, then one would most likely be socially rejected.

Why is it that the same cultural practice exhibited in a different context could be seen as inappropriate? For instance, some have been raised with the idea that the young should not speak unless spoken to. Despite whatever good opinion an individual has, one must not talk back to an adult. Some who grow up with this kind of philosophy would appear inhibited or even socially dysfunctional in a context that requires constant response and feedback. Thus, in a different social context, a person could be judged to be timid or even lacking courage or backbone, when one practices what one perceives and was taught to be deference to those who are older than him.

How is it that his not talking back and not speaking before being spoken to, like he was taught in his youth, come to be a standard to judge his whole character as weak and his person as having some kind of social problems? It's the new context in which he finds himself. In the new cultural and social setting, one should talk back and even speak up even before being asked to talk. The ability to do this will judge him as a normal member of that society and as someone who could function as a viable member of that society. His behavior has not changed but the standards by which he is judged has. And this is because people back home held different values about the concept of courage, normalcy, and what is proper. But in the minds of those participating in judgment and social conviction of the young man, they were making assessment based on what is an absolute standard in the new society.

What the social judges in the new context do not recognize is that in the minds of those back home -- that is, of the young, socially-convicted man -- they also have absolute standards and rules to judge by. If a person from the new environment made a voyage to the young man's home and acted in the way that was normal in the previous context, such as freely speaking even when not spoken to and also being quick to respond to statements, the members of the community will judge him harshly as one who is rude and talks back to his elders. So, a perfectly normal individual in one society will be deemed socially dysfunctional in another society. Culture and its values are certainly context bound in many cases.

In the context of the water park, almost everyone was wearing a swimsuit. After all, all the rides involved getting wet and even almost full emersion in water. There was even an artificial tidal wave at the center of the park. Many loved it because it had the element of fun that tidal waves of Atlantic Ocean afforded without the messiness of sand nor the danger of being swept away into the sea to a possible last journey. Perhaps, in the context of the water park, it would have been somewhat awkward to be fully dressed. I couldn't spot even one person without some kind of swimsuit or water-friendly clothing.

Even without the gambling, waiting to see who gets the most wet with clothes on, aspect of the rolling rapid water ride, we were all happy to be getting on it. It was a fun ride, period. My two friends were talking to each other when they stepped into the boat and so they ended up sitting next to each other. I was quite happy with the developments. They were going to be body to body in that ride.

They have been enjoying a good conversation for a while, and, now, there's even the fun element of water thrown into the equation. Even the winds seemed favorable to our boat journey.

But I immediately saw a disturbing thing. My male friend quickly became taciturn, and I could see that he was even turning red. Maybe he was getting excited sitting next to my very attractive female friend. She had the sweetest smile in the world. She looked really cute with her blue bikini complementing her blue eyes. Her golden hair formed a suggestive curl in its wetness, and it flowed and landed in an excited way on her shoulders. Her skin was nicely tanned and looked smooth. He must have been feeling her skin at every point where his body touched hers. The seats were not very big, and they, after all, even shared a seat belt, so there was quite a bit of necessary touching. I don't think my friend was complaining, but he was definitely struck dumb, quickly. I saw my female friend noticing that, too. I was thinking of things to say to help him jump start the conversation in the new setting. But they had already secured their seat belt, and I wasn't even properly seated, yet. I and my talking companion had to go to the other side of the boat because all the seats close to the entrance were taken. My two friends were already securely seated in a coupled seat near the entrance way.

The operator of the rolling rapid ride seemed a little impatient. Who could blame him? There was a long line with endless number of people. He didn't have a cold drink full of ice to keep him cool. And these rides teased him as he was consciously reminded that he was missing out. He was one of the few people who was fully dressed. Granted, he had shorts and a T-shirt with the water park picture and name on it. Still, he stuck out like a sore thumb amidst all the bikinis and swimming trunks. I wanted to be considerate to him and to the rest of the riders of our rolling rapids vehicle, so I concentrated on sitting down.

The seats were really small and close together. I came to know what my friend must have been feeling. My traveling companion's bare skin was forcing its way onto my skin as we tried to put the single seat belt around the both of us. I would not have been surprised if I were as red as my friend over there. As my talking companion helped to put the seat belt around us, I smelled her perfume. It had a nice flowery smell. I noticed how beautiful her green eyes were. She had long eye lashes and the cutest nose in the world. I liked how her lips looked; it was full but petite in size. Her lips fit really well with her small facial and body frame. She had long brunette hair, and it was forming curly locks at the bottom right on the top of her shoulders and even her upper arm. Some of her hair touched my face while she was fastening the seat belt. She was wearing a bright pink bikini, which accentuated her nicely tanned skin. This bikini did not have straps, but I could see a lighter, although still tan, strap line. I wondered how she would look in that other bikini. She certainly looked really good in what she was wearing.

When we were sitting so close together like this, I almost forgot what was going on with my two friends. I thought to myself, what was I doing concentrating on what the two of my friends were talking about? I was next to this lovely lady whom I could get to know. I was sure that my two friends could take care of themselves. From then on, I seemed not to hear what two of my friends were talking about as I concentrated on talking with my sitting partner. At the end of the ride, all of us were really wet. We were not displeased since our cold sodas were all gone, and the sun seemed to be shining at its height. I, on my part, have to confess that some bodily heat of my own was created during the ride. Who could have imagined that there was so much heat to go around in this world?

The day ended really well, and we parted. I was happy that I was able to exchange telephone numbers with Katie. From the wild rafting ride onwards, I concentrated on getting to know Katie better. In fact, Katie and I parted company with our friends. We used the excuse that we wanted to ride the water rafting ride once again. My two friends, I knew, did not like to do anything over again. This was something they certainly shared, so I knew that they were not going to stand in line again. I didn't know what Katie's position was on this, but I threw out the suggestion looking at her. She seemed to catch the hint, and I was excited that she wanted to do the same. As expected, my other two friends did not want to go on the ride, again.

It wasn't all selfishness on my part. I was hoping that this would afford them time alone to get to know each other better and even get more personal with each other. Since I thought that my two friends had the maximum possible number of opportunities available to them during the time that they were alone, I was distressed to find that my friend did not even get her phone number. He didn't even indicate in any clear way that he liked her, romantically. What made the whole situation upsetting was the fact that he was really attracted to her. He admitted this to me that very night. To add tragedy to the whole story, I found out later from Katie that her friend was very attracted to my friend. If he had made any romantic gestures, she would have accepted, and they would now be an item.

But I also found out from Katie that her friend lost interest in my friend and was upset that he made no efforts to contact her. Katie told me that her friend's pride was hurt, so there was no way that my friend and her best friend could now become an item, barring some cupid's magic arrow. I told Katie that I thought this was utterly stupid because she was attracted to him, and she was possibly passing up great happiness. Katie responded with the statement that girls are stupid and guys are dumb. I was dumbfounded by her response, so I asked her for clarification.

Katie said that girls were stupid because they think that guys catch the hints that they send and think that guys should know what they are doing. This presupposition often gets in the way of their gaining happiness and the boyfriend of their choice. And the guys, Katie added, were dumb because they just can't catch the hints that women send out and, often, they just don't get it. Katie explained that guys don't know how to maneuver through the romantic waves often fraught with secret tests and storms. Guys think that they just need to go straight, and everything will work out. Now, Katie exclaimed, that's dumb!

I didn't want Pierre to be like my other friend or be in the category of the dumb and confirm Katie's formula. I was resolved not to lose focus. I was going to be there for Pierre every step of the way to see his relationship with Orli being in the realm of a joyous and happy relationship and not imprisoned to the realm of friendship, in which two of them have romantic interests but could never share that with each other. What greater prison could there be?

Since Pierre and I had a dinner invitation the following week from Orit and Orli, there was actually one week hiatus to think and talk about the question. How can Pierre take hold of the opportunity that presented itself to him? This could be the most important moment of his life. It's possible that he will find the happiness that he's been searching for. Orli could be the one who will play an important part in that regard, since it was obvious that Pierre has fallen for Orli. If Pierre really wanted the romance with Orli to happen, then Pierre had to make some kind of romantic gesture or invitation for only two of them to go out together. The next few days were going to be filled with brainstorming for ideas to bring this about. I was going to be there for Pierre to bounce off his ideas. And whatever help I could extend in terms of providing ideas and strategies, I was going to be there for Pierre.

9

Soul Mate?

Next several days, we were quite curious about how the dinner would be. Perhaps, our frustration at coming up with creative ideas for Pierre to transition from a developing friendship to a romantic relationship spurred our curiosity even further. Also, there was a bit of a foreigner's curiosity in each of us. We were not familiar with too many local Israeli food dishes. This did not mean that Pierre and I did not eat quite a bit of Israeli food. We often ate falafel for lunch. They are relatively inexpensive. For about a-dollar-and-a-half equivalent in shekels, one could get about three falafel balls, grounded chickpea mixture rolled up into a small ball and then deep fried in oil. These are placed inside a pita, Middle Eastern bread that is circular. There is an air pocket in the middle that allows one to stuff things, such as falafel balls and vegetables, inside. Because of the way the bread is cooked, its air pocket is basically completely sealed off. So, one cut off a small plateau at a round side in order to stuff the pita with edible goodies. Falafel is placed inside the pita bread, often, along with salads stuffed inside.

My favorite salad is the one made of egg plants, which are thinly sliced and then fried with garlic. My other favorite salad is composed of long green peppers that are fried in olive oil. After being cooked, they are soft in

texture but retained their quite spicy taste.
Other salads that are often found in these
falafel shops are good as well, such as potato
or carrot salads. There are also pickles and
pickled vegetables that one can place in the
pita with falafel balls. Some places have salads
out in the open, so that one who purchased the
falafel -- the term used to refer also to the pita
with falafel balls inside -- can go and stuff as
much of his favorite salad or as many different
salads as he wants.

Besides the salads, there are several
different kinds of sauces. There is the most
basic, or rather fundamental, sauce, called
humus. Normally, humus is a spread, and it's
certainly sold as such in the USA. But often,
falafel shops thin the thick humus spread with
water, so that it is basically a liquid, and one
can pour some over the falafel balls and salads
inside the pita pocket. Some falafel shops have
the liquid humus in addition to the paste
humus, which they rub onto the inside of the
pita pockets before they throw the falafel balls
inside.

Many Israelis adore the taste of humus,
one Israeli friend of mine explained to me, and
that is why the stores with all-you-can-use
liquid humus sometimes attract more customers. One can have as much additional
humus applied to the falafel as possible. In
most places, there is a greater variety of sauces

than just the humus. There's tahinah, which is also white in color, but more tangy and sharp in taste. My favorite sauce is the shuhug, which is quite spicy in nature. Shuhug comes in two different colors, red and green. They are both really spicy. Although I know that there's a difference between the two, I am not able to tell that difference. I apply shuhug whenever possible, so if anyone can tell the difference, I feel that I should be able to.

Shuhug is really good. But, the spiciness of the sauce renders a can of Diet Coke ineffective. The stuff is that spicy. When I know that I am going to apply a generous portion of shuhug, I make sure that I purchase a half liter bottle of Diet Coke. Another sauce that I have come to appreciate more and more with each passing visit to Israeli food stands is Amba. It's a yellowish sauce made from mango. It is exotic in the sense that I was not previously familiar with the taste. At first, it felt a little too strong. But as time went on, its taste came to complement the shuhug taste. I came to feel that amba is just as indispensable as shuhug. Amba is not as common as humus or even shuhug in Israeli food stands or shops where falafel is found. In a short time, the existence of amba became a final arbiter as to whether I was going to frequent the food stand or not.

Besides falafel, I often have swarma for lunch. The concept of the food is the same with falafel. Swarma is made of meat combination of lamb and turkey, but which even included other meats as well. It is roasted in a machine that has a vertical pole in the middle and an electric grill at one of the sides. The meat is punctured by the vertical pole in the middle and spun slowly around with the rotating pole through the middle of the meat while being heated and roasted. One often sees raw meat turning golden brown and appetizing in appearance. Frequently, the owner of the store cuts off thin pieces from the surface of the large meat matter when the swarma looks a golden brown color and gathers the thinly sliced pieces below in a container, allowing the deeper meat to have their chance at turning brown. Slices of the swarma meat gathered in the container are placed inside a pita pocket with salads added, and then the whole inside is showered in sauces.

I prefer swarma because of its taste, primarily. In terms of protein value, falafel and swarma may compete pretty well. Of course, I am not a nutritionist and am guided by popular perception in these matters. One other popular perception is, sometimes, a motivation for consuming swarma as well. According to conventional Israeli wisdom, falafel produces flatulence. I don't think that this is totally inaccurate. If I have to be totally honest, I have to say that I have personal experiences to back it up. I also have had the experience of participating in the falafel-flatulence process of Pierre as the perpetrator.

Although flatulence is flatulence and it smells bad whether I am the originator or Pierre, somehow it always seemed to smell worse when Pierre was the one engaged in the falafel-flatulence process. Often, when Pierre and I were together for lunch, I tried to steer him away from falafel to swarma. I was rarely successful since Pierre loved falafel. I learned to adapt to the situation, and with an acceptance of the inevitable, I opened windows and checked for smooth airflow. Also, I invested in another freshner, this time for our room. We had one for the bathroom. I tried to be as inconspicuous as possible in order to make Pierre not feel so uncomfortable after letting it out. However, too often, Pierre pretended like he did not flatulate. As it happened, these flatulences were silent in nature, and what was absent in sound made up in smell. I wished that Pierre warned me either before, during, or after he flatulated, so that I could take out my air freshner. I was going to find out for certain, anyway. It was a small room after all.

Although I was quite annoyed that Pierre did not inform me of his flatulence, I also recognized that it's an embarrassing thing for him. This knowledge made it more difficult to dispel the smell, because I did not want to hurt Pierre's feelings. Often, I gently reached over to the freshner and spray it as inconspicuously as possible and pretended like nothing happened the way Pierre did. But my good intentioned efforts rarely succeeded because the aerosol spray almost never failed to make a noise. After a while, though, we got used to the falafel-flatulence and aerosol-diffusion process. It was perhaps a necessary side effect of consuming food that gave us much pleasure, so we were more than willing to put up with it, Pierre more than I.

Pierre and I were hoping that, at the upcoming dinner, we were going to have the opportunity to try some Israeli food that we haven't already tried, so that we could add to the list of our favorite foods a few more dishes besides falafel and swarma. We were not sure what we could expect from the dinner. I didn't think that Orit and Orli were going to make falafel and swarma. First of all, swarma was quite difficult to make since one needed an instrument with which to roast the meat. Also, I didn't know where one could purchase meat for swarma. I didn't see any meat labeled as swarma in the Jerusalem Market Place or in the supermarkets. Falafel also didn't seem like a possible candidate. Falafel could be more easily made, but it was quite ubiquitous in Israel. I figured that they would want to make food that was less common. Orit and Orli impressed me as sensitive individuals in that way, who cared that Pierre and I experience new and different things in their country. I was not going to be surprised if the food they prepared had a special significance, since both Pierre and I shared how the dishes that we prepared had special, personal meaning for us. In a way, our sharing ourselves through our dishes formed a cornerstone for our dinner conversation and an essential connection conduit with Orit and Orli on a personal level.

Cooking our food and sharing our personal experiences with Orit and Orli, in fact, became ritualized. Telling a story attach-ed to food and having Orit and Orli participate in our experiences by listening to us became sacred to us. Pierre and I marked that moment in time as sacred time in which we were personally invested. We were allowing Orit and Orli into our world and making ourselves vulnerable to them. It was a way in which we extended our past experiences to Orit and Orli on a silver platter and implicitly asked them to consider becoming our experiences of the future. Although not verbalized in that manner, I felt that Orit and Orli understood.

They participated in our memory and shared with us what was personal to them.

They wanted the ritual of sharing and empa-
thetic experience to continue, and that was
why they decided to invite us for dinner. This
was the deeper meaning behind their ready
dinner invitation even before the first dinner
together ended. They were excited to experience our sacred space and time, and they
wanted us to be a part of their sacred space
and time. Although it was not always easy to
invite a person to one's sacred place and time
since it renders the initiator more vulnerable,
there's a therapeutic and even redemptive
element to initiating others into one's sacred
space and time. Orit and Orli wanted to
experience the other side of the experience.
They were the initiates in our meal fellowship;
now, they wanted to be the initiators.

Of course, on a simple level, they enjoyed having dinner with us and our company,
so they wanted to invite us over and continue
that. But Platonic interpretation is often
helpful in assessing the true reality of things.
Perhaps, ultimate reality of things. Often, what
we see are shadows of reality. True reality lies
deep within. In this simple formula of Platonic
thought, I could say that the idea of Orit and
Orli inviting us for dinner because they
enjoyed it was a reflection of the deeper reality.
The true reality was that they wanted to
continue the deeper connection of vicarious
experience in sacred space and time. Of

course, at this stage, it's only a theoretical assessment -- a hypothesis, if you will. But it was a hypothesis based on a forming formula.

Both Pierre and I enjoyed the dinner on a superficial level, but after an inner probing of why we enjoyed the dinner so much, we came to see the deeper reality. It began with a simple statement, such as, I felt comfortable with them. I felt like I connected. Then, the question of why we felt that way was raised. The answer to the question lay in the fact that we were given the opportunity to share with them something that was deeply personal to us. There was a reciprocation in that they were willing to share their personal opinions and deep thoughts with us. This was a process, a form of ritual. In an unconscious way, we not only invited Orit and Orli into our apartments, but into our hearts. And the fact that Orit and Orli invited us over to their apartment for dinner was not merely for the sake of eating. It was Orit and Orli's way of inviting us into their lives and even perhaps their hearts. The visible, superficial reality, or the shadow, was that they were inviting us for dinner. The inner or truer reality was that they were inviting us into their lives and hearts.

So, the question of what they were going to make for us to eat transcended beyond culinary interest. Concern with cuisine reflected the shadow of our real interest.

Deeper reality of our verbalized question lay in the question of what we thought Orit and Orli were going to share with us, in terms of their personal life. We initiated them into our sacred time and space, and they participated in the ritual that we created for them. Will Orit and Orli initiate us proactively into their sacred space and sacred time -- a place in their heart and experience that was very personal and important to them? Will Orit and Orli share to the extent that they bare themselves vulnerable to us? Deeper reality of our ques-tions were eventually verbalized in a com-fortable and, even, usual way.

This is not to say that we were not genuinely interested in the dishes for their own sake. Like the next guy, Pierre and I appre-ciated good food. Good food certainly brought more than a modicum amount of happiness. But it was certainly different from questioning the quality or diversity of food before going to a restaurant. Technically, we could go to any Israeli restaurant and try new foods. Perhaps, the deeper reality was more relevant in this case because we were interested in Orit and Orli in a personal way. Pierre was roman-tically interested in Orli. Even the term, head over heels, might not be inappropriate to describe the state that Pierre was in.

For myself, I knew that I was deeply attracted to Orit. I could not say, though, that I was head over heels for her. I didn't have a heart beating in an amplified way when I saw her. Of course, I was using the Pierre Rule for finding someone who is a possible soul mate. This guideline could be totally wrong. Although the jury was out on love, I knew that I was interested in Orit and very much attracted to her. I certainly desired to get involved with Orit in a more romantic way. I knew that Pierre felt that there was a large stake in the upcoming dinner, and, somehow, I shared his concern, certainly for him but even for myself. And, so, it went. With questions regarding what kind of dish we thought Orit and Orli were going to make, we were contemplating possibilities that could certainly alter our experiences in Israel and even our lives.

10

The Daughter
of the Sea

Soon enough, the day arrived, although it felt like it would never arrive. Both Pierre and I were quite excited about the possibilities that lay ahead. We wondered what the day was going to bring for us. We had more questions than answers, and the questions seemed to have multiplied with each passing day since the dinner meeting with Orit and Orli in our humble abode. Now, we were approaching the Orit and Orli castle, and we were not sure how we might be princes on white horses and in shining armor. Orit and Orli were certainly tough, so if anyone was going to be on a white horse with a shining armor, Pierre and I felt that Orit and Orli surely could be. It wasn't that we were not tough, but there seemed to be almost an Amazon quality about Orit and Orli. It wasn't because they were not feminine and unat-tractive. On the contrary, they were very beautiful.

For me at least, my first image of Orit was with her in her army outfit and brandishing a M16. At that moment, if any-thing happened which required saving people, I would not have doubted that Orit would have done an efficient job in the way that she was trained in the Israeli Defense Forces. This image was engraved in my mind, and even in Orit's most feminine moments and form, that image destroyed any traditional gender category in which I was culturally conditioned in the USA. Before Orit came for the dinner, I think that I did an effective job describing to Pierre how Orit looked -- my first impressions of a beautiful army girl with a gentle smile -- that Pierre shared my confusion and could not honestly subscribe to the familiar gender distinctions and the usual characterizations of men and women extant in the West. Pierre did not personally see Orit with a M16, but he did see enough young women with M16 in daily public life that he was able to relate fully to my description.

So, there we were going over to Orit and Orli not as knights in shining armor, but as just regular guys. The fact that Orit and Orli seemed to upset gender categories that we were used to perhaps made it more difficult to see how we might approach them romantically. It's more than possible that we were overthinking the situation and creating questions that needed not to be raised. However, this questioning might, at least in small part, be attributed to culture shock.

Pierre and I never discussed the topic of culture shock until that very moment that we stood outside Orit and Orli's door about to ring the bell. But it struck me at that moment that Pierre and I were experiencing culture shock of sorts. We were experiencing differences in cultures in a deeply personal way. It required a personal issue to bring this realization to the fore. How much more personal can one get than in one's romantic affection for someone else? Pierre was deeply desirous of a relationship with Orli, and what should have been an easy answer to the question of how we might bring this to fruition became a philosophical treatise without any real answers. Sure, there's the difficulty of transitioning from a possible friendship to a relationship, but even there, the answer was not so difficult. One had simply to make sure that the romantic intent became explicit. It can be done with words or gestures. Pierre could have easily asked Orli out for coffee or something so that they could get to know each other better on a one-to-one basis. But all these practical steps and fairly easy answers to what Pierre should do seemed to have evaded us in the past few days.

Pierre not being able to think clearly about this can be explained in part by his strong feelings for Orli, but my not being able to provide clear answers to Pierre even as a third party certainly can be attributed in part to cultural factors that I was trying to wade through. In a way, there were too many inputs, and within a short period of a week, it wasn't the easiest thing to provide clear answers to the question engulfed in culture shock. Recognizing culture shock as an impediment to our clear thinking had the effect of making the solution look simpler. Simply, the fact remained that for Pierre and Orli to be together, they had to share a romantic moment together. There had to be something that transitioned them into the romantic realm, whether it be a kiss, holding hands, putting arm around each other, or any other such gesture. For this to happen, there had to be right romantic conditions, such as Pierre and Orli having the opportunity to be together alone and getting to know each other better. If Pierre really wanted this to happen, he just had to ask. So, right before Pierre rang the bell, I stopped him by telling Pierre to wait one second. I didn't want to stand in front of Orit and Orli's door way and carry on a whole discussion, so I told Pierre succinctly that if he wanted Orli, then he should find an opportunity to ask Orli to go out for drinks. Pierre looked at me, so I gave him a reassuring gaze and asked him, Okay? Pierre looked at me nervously but said he would. He seemed to tense up incrementally, so I told him that I bet Orli and Orit will look amazing tonight. That brought a smile to Pierre's face, so I rang the door bell.

And sure enough, Orit and Orli looked fantastic. But before I could properly savor their beauty, I was immediately seized by the sweet odor coming from their kitchen. It felt as if I were transposed in another place and time.

It smelled of spices with which I was not familiar. The sweet aroma held no memories for me personally because it was new to me. This was not the case with familiar smell of food. When I smelled pepperoni pizza, I remembered the first bite of my pepperoni pizza with mom and dad. I even vaguely remembered the street where I had the first bite of that pizza. I didn't recall all the details, but the sweet odor of pepperoni pizza, my favorite pizza, seemed always to bring back the taste of the first pizza bite.

There were other memories attached to pepperoni pizza. I remember going out for pepperoni pizza after little league games, particularly when we won. I remember the coach. He didn't look particularly athletic. In fact, he's a professor at a local college and always brought a book with him to the prac- tices and games. But I never saw him reading the books that he brought with him. Maybe, the book was a security blanket for him. I remember dad telling me that the coach was a respected professor and scholar. To this day, I don't know what his expertise is. I know that he taught some kind of literature. A large part of the reason why I don't know what he taught was because he never discussed his work. The coach talked only about baseball. During practices, he was focused on trying to get us to be best players. And even when we went out for pepperoni pizza after the game, he talked about the game. When not talking about our games, he interjected a baseball story or jokes about baseball.

Despite his total focus on baseball, we didn't seem to win very much. Although it did not bother most of us that we didn't win a championship, I felt that it did bother the coach a bit. I understand that he still coaches the same little league. I am told that the team has not won a championship, yet. Being grown up, I often wonder in passing about what kind of professor he is. I would not be surprised if he is a great scholar who's used to winning in scholarship. I guess he wanted to replicate the star performance with his little league team. It was the coach's intense focus on winning and visible disappointment at not winning that caused me to never really have him among my life's role models. I liked the coach a lot and still have only fond memories of him. But there's certainly more to life than winning. In this regard, I have dad as a role model. His motto was to strive best for everything but enjoy what you do. Dad added that the most important thing in the process is doing good. Even as a grown up, I feel that there's more value in such a philosophy.

Food is often a memory capsule. Smell and taste often conjure up memories, both positive and negative. Food is a supplement to one's life story and often a vital player in it, whether one recognizes this actively or not. It is no surprise, therefore, that food plays a central role in so many religious ceremonies. Sometimes, an active attribution of significance is attached to foods in a religious ceremony or celebration. Other times, food provided in religious contexts comes to have meaning on their own. This can be seen as a passive attribution of meaning. What I mean by this is that it's not the specific nature of food that gives meaning to the food; rather, the religiosity of the event is the significant factor. Food is secondary in importance and can often, in theory, be replaced by another. However, secondary factors sometimes become fixed in ritual, so this is not always possible in practice.

An example of an active attribution of meaning to food is the wine in the Passover seder. The wine itself is very important and one cannot really replace it with, say, milk and have the same significance. A part of the reason is that the significance of wine for the seder is textually bound. There are religious texts that instruct and record use of wine for the seder. An example of a passive attribution of meaning is the main course used in a Friday evening Shabbat meal. One could serve beef or lamb and they would have the same extent of significance in the context of a religious practice. There is not a specific instruction as to what exact dish one must serve. The religious significance is actively attributed not to a particular food or drink in this case, but to the event itself. What food is served is ancillary in the ritual.

In the same way that food has an active or passive significance in a religious ceremony or celebration, food plays a primary or secondary function for activities that might not be deemed religious, as well. This is because there is a ritualization to all aspects of human behavior. One can call someting a secular or mundane ritual, but it is a ritual, nonetheless.

For instance, having lunch is a ritual. Better put, eating lunch becomes ritualized in human society. The nominal term, *ritual*, pinpoints the final product; whereas, the verbal term, *ritualized*, highlights the process. There are several aspects to ritualization. Sometimes, we eat lunch alone. Other times, we eat lunch with a friend. And in other instances, we have lunch that involves some kind of business. All three types of lunch eating experience are rituals of one sort or another. Eating alone can be seen with the primary function of food consumption, most likely necessitated by a need to eat, or hunger. Eating lunch together with a friend might not have as its primary function food consumption. It is possible that the primary purpose of eating is to bond with the friend. This may be

The Daughter of the Sea

understandable in appearance, say, by a third person observer looking at an involved conversation between the participants of the meal. Eating itself may only be a small part of that bonding process and may only provide a background context to that particular meal ritual. In the third case, that of the business lunch, it has as its purpose making of a business deal, either in the short run or in the long run. In this light, the context of where one will eat or bring one's client is an important factor to the lunch ritual. All aspects of the meal are geared toward making the deal come through. Perhaps, it is in the business meal that the setting and food play the most central role because they are meant to produce the final result of a business deal.

The precise ritual nature of the second dinner together for the four of us, Pierre, Orit, Orli, and me, was not clearly defined. So, it was somewhat unsettling that I was now in a room with aroma that was completely foreign to me. I did not quite know what to expect that night. I had a good feeling about it, however, and the pleasantness of new food odors certainly played an important role in creating this intuition. I was eager to try new things and quite curious about what stories these dishes contained.

Before long, we were all sitting around the dinner table. Orit and Orli's apartment was basically the same in structure and space allotment as ours, so it didn't take long for us to settle down into our seats and be comfortably ready for our table fellowship. Orit opened the wine bottle that we brought. Soon, our glasses were filled, and a toast was said for our happiness. It was a simple toast but one that seemed just right. And then came the appetizer. It was soup. I was told that it was Matza Ball soup. Pierre seemed to be somewhat familiar with this soup. For me, it was certainly the first time trying the soup. I generally like soup, so I was excited at the site of the soup before me and was quite eager to try this new soup. I might add it in my unofficial list of my favorite soups, after all.

I like soup of all kinds, but my particular favorite is New England Clam Chowder. I like the creamy nature of the soup. It is wonderful to taste the creamy milky flavor and the vegetable broth as the soup makes its way down to the stomach. And the vegetables seem to be so perfect in its place within the soup. Taking a bite and chewing on vegetables with the flavor of the creamy soup pervading through the vegetables is a culinary ecstasy. As the soft potatoes melt in the mouth, I would dip my soup spoon deep into the clam chowder soup and bring it back with vegetables laden with the creamy soup. Of course, the best part of the New England Clam

Chowder is the clams. Having fresh clams and abundance of it in the soup makes the soup either a first rate clam chowder soup or a second rate clam chowder soup. The flavor of the soup can do only so much to making the soup a quality soup. Especially since the name distinctively states that it's a clam chowder soup and not a potato chowder soup, not having many clams seems like a breach of contract. If they wanted to give customers soup mostly with vegetables with one or two pieces of clams, it seems dishonest to call it a clam chowder soup. A clam chowder should, first and foremost, have lots of clams.

Clams within New England Clam Chowder Soup can be heavenly. Marinated with the creamy soup broth for who knows how long, each clam morsel has the distinctive taste of the broth. If the soup taste is good, then one can bet that the clam pieces will certainly bear testimony to that. What's great also about clam pieces inside the clam chowder is that while brazening the sweet taste of the chowder, the clams keep their distinctive clam taste as well. Thus, in effect, clams have their distinctive self-contained seasoning that complements the taste of the broth. And the texture of clams one feels as one chews the morsel is an experience. Clams are not mushy; they have a distinctive chew. It makes one feel like one is actually eating something and not just eating a pseudo-solid matter. With every bite, unique clam taste pervades through the taste buds and accentuates culinary pleasure initiated by the creamy chowder broth taste. It is, in fact, this part of chewing the clams while consuming the clam chowder soup process that is the epitome, or climax, of the New England Clam Chowder Soup Experience.

In Israel, I did not spot New England Clam Chowder Soup in any of the restaurants that I had a chance to visit. It might be due partly to the fact that clam is unkosher, or ritually impure, according to observant Judaism. Many restaurants serve kosher food, and some restaurants proudly display the certificate of kashrut in a visible place. This does not mean that there are not unkosher restaurants. In Jerusalem, in the Midrahov, the most popular street for restaurants, I walked inside one place and saw pork chops on the menu. Anyone who knows anything about what is kosher and what is not knows that pork is certainly not kosher. This is not the only restaurant in Jerusalem serving pork products. I heard from a friend that there is a place where one can get a good bacon cheese burger in Jerusalem.

How can one explain why there are pork products in restaurants, but it is hard to find New England Clam Chowder? One answer that I conjectured relates to availability.

There are Israeli pig farms that export to foreign countries. I even heard of a kibbutz, whose primary business is pig farming. It would not be difficult for restaurants to tag into this market source, if they choose to. I don't think, however, that there is an active clam farming business in Israel. If restaurants have to import clams in order to serve them in a clam chowder soup, there's the question of the cost. It may be too expensive. There's also the question of freshness. What makes a New England Clam Chowder soup truly great is the abundance of clams and the freshness of them. For clams to be imported, they may not be so fresh when they finally reach the restaurants. The risk of having expensively imported clams go bad may discourage any restaurant owner from taking that risk. So, while being in Israel, I have been in search of a favorite soup that was readily available.

Matza Ball soup wasn't so readily available in restaurants either, but French Onion soup was. First time that Pierre and I went to a restaurant, he ordered a French Onion soup. Pierre went on and on about the merits of the soup. I had never tried French Onion soup before. In the USA, I always ordered a clam chowder soup whenever I got the chance. When there were no clam chowder soup, I chose a chicken soup or a goulash soup over French Onion soup. But with Pierre's high recommendations for its merits, I decided to try the French Onion soup. It was really good. That particular soup, Pierre told me, was especially good. There were quite a bit of onion pieces inside and a big piece of melted cheese on top.

The taste of cheese mixed in with onion pieces made a nice harmonious taste. The tanginess of onion and the blandness of cheese provided a ying-and-yang to the taste balance. Even in terms of texture, there seemed to be opposition that set the onion pieces and cheese in a harmonious balance. Onion pieces were easily disjointed and broken up inside the soup and inside one's mouth. Melted cheese, on the other hand, seemed to cohere together as a single whole in the soup. It took a bit of work to break them apart for consumption. Cheese seemed to hold tenaciously to the soup spoon as well when one worked to put the piece in one's mouth. More often than not, pieces of cheese left a receipt on the spoon. Even inside one's mouth, the melted cheese felt like it was clinging to one's teeth. There was none of that struggle with the onion pieces. There was simply no resistance. Its journey from the soup bowl to the stomach was smooth and a willing one.

From that time on, Pierre and I made a small game of finding the best French Onion soup in Israel. So, in order to find our answer,

we tried French Onion soup at every restaurant that we had a chance to visit. The
verdict still is that the first restaurant has the
best French Onion soup. Since we always have
French Onion soup in restaurants, we didn't
get to try too many other kinds of soup. In
fact, this Matza Ball soup is the first non-
French Onion soup that we tasted in Israel.

As Pierre and I savored the taste of the
Matza Ball soup, Orit said that the soup is
usually made during Passover. Orit and Orli
made the soup because they wanted us to
share their experience. Orli said she consumed
quite a bit of the soup during the course of her
life as each Passover passed. I felt privileged to
participate in Orit's life experience. I liked the
taste of the soup, so I asked for seconds. I
asked Orit, if she would teach me how to make
it, sometime. Orit gave me an answer, first,
with her smile and, then, with a verbal yes. I
was glad because, now, we had an opportunity
to get together to share something together. It
could be a kind of a date. I thought that it
would be pretty intimate making food together. It would give us an opportunity to get
to know each other better through conversation, while creating a culinary delight,
together. Not only that, since it would be just
Orit and me, it could be quite romantic,
sharing the fruits of our labors together. I

resolved then to create this opportunity in a not-too-distant future.

Asking Orit to teach me how to make Matza Ball soup reminded me about the recipe. I took out the neatly written recipe for the fried vegetables. I made two copies -- one for Orit and other for Orli. I told them as I handed the recipes to them that I would be happy to make the dish with them. I made a point of looking at Orit longer than Orli and even ending my sentence while looking at Orit so that my interest in Orit would be clear. I had a concern for Pierre and his desire as well, so I didn't want to send any mixed signals. I wanted to do all that I could to facilitate Pierre's search for happiness with Orli. Supporting my friend in his quest was very important for me.

I was happy to see that Orit responded quickly to my invitation by saying that, maybe, we could do that when we get together to make the Matza Ball soup together. I was also glad for Pierre to see that Orli looked at him and smiled when Orit was speaking. I thought it was a way in which Orli was encouraging and reassuring Pierre of her interest in him.

I wondered what was going through Pierre's mind. Pierre made some pleasant and polite comments about the soup, but he seemed a little bit more taciturn than usual and certainly more so than the last time we had dinner together with Orit and Orli. Perhaps,

Pierre was nervous thinking about asking Orli out for some time alone together. It seemed to me that Orli would say, yes, to whatever Pierre asked since it was clear that Orli was interested in Pierre. I felt that I should try to encourage Pierre, somehow.

With these thoughts in mind, I beheld what looked like some bite sized morsels wrapped in green leaves. The dish that Orli brought out was aesthetically beautiful. These green-leaf-covered, bite-sized food items were stacked in the form of a pyramid. They looked quite appetizing. I let out a small exclamation of pleasure. Pierre followed suit with his expression almost of bewilderment. Pierre looked genuinely excited at the site of the food pyramid. I knew, then, that I did not need to come to Pierre's rescue. Pierre was looking very comfortable and genuinely interested in the content of the food. Pierre asked Orli what the food was. Orli was all smiles. Orli was obviously happy that even before we tasted her dish, we were both mesmerized by it. In my opinion, her excitement was added by the interest that Pierre was taking in her dish.

Orli began her narrative on how this dish was important to her. Orli recounted to Pierre and me that the dish was a signature dish of her grandmother, who immigrated to Israel from Syria. There was a small Jewish community in Syria several decades ago, and most of the Jews of that community already were in Israel as immigrants. This Jewish community, according to Orli, spoke Arabic but also Aramaic. I had thought that Aramaic was a dead language only found in parts of the Bible. The original text of Daniel is largely preserved in Biblical Aramaic in contrast to the rest of the Old Testament, which is preserved in Biblical Hebrew. So, I expressed my surprise that Aramaic was still being spoken by some people. Orli commented that not only was Aramaic spoken among Jews in Syria, but that there were Syrian Christians who communicated in an Aramaic dialect of their own. I was quite fascinated and was curious about these communities. But I did not want my historical and linguistic interest to hinder Orli's recounting of the significance of the dish for her, personally. So, I kept silent and repressed all my questions.

Orli said that her grandmother taught her mom how to make this dish, composed of rice inside grape leaves. Orli recounted that her mother learned to make the dish so well that people always asked for it when they came to a party at their parent's home. And it's often the first dish to disappear, always towards the beginning of the party. This seemed to be the case no matter how much her mom made them. Orli added that it was this very dish that played the cupid's arrow in making her dad fall in love with her mom. Both her mom and dad told Orli this. Orli confessed that it was actually because of this testimonial, that she was motivated to learn to make the dish. Orli gave a lighthearted laughter afterwards, signaling to us that it was, at least, partly a joke. We both smiled. Orit said that Orli took a long time to make the dish because the grape leaves had to be soft enough to wrap the rice inside and to be consumed. Despite the seemingly simple ingredients of rice and grape leaves, the process was fairly complicated. There were various spices that were used to give it a distinctive and characteristic taste.

Pierre responded by thanking Orli for sharing this special dish with us. I was glad that Pierre took the leadership in thanking Orli. Orli seemed to be quite flattered. I noticed her face turning a little red. Certainly a good sign, I thought. Orli served all of us three grape-leaf-wrapped food pieces and put the remaining batch in the middle of the table. The first bite was like nothing I had ever tasted before. It had a slight tangy taste, and I could taste various spices as well. It was wonderful. I knew with my first bite that I would be forever bonded to this grape-leaf dish. Pierre seemed to love the dish as well. I haven't seen Pierre eat so quickly before.

Even before I reached my third piece, Pierre was done with all three of his and was asking Orli if he could take a few more. Pierre always faulted on the side of being overly polite. Orli seemed happy that Pierre was so eager to have more but that he deferred to her for permission. Orli volunteered to put four more onto Pierre's plate. Pierre thanked her and continued to consume the grape-leaf morsels, no doubt falling more and more in love with Orli. I am a witness to the fact that Pierre fell in love with Orli before he ever tasted her dish, but, certainly, I could see that this dish just gave Pierre more excuses to elevate Orli in his heart.

I helped myself to a few more pieces of the good stuff, as well. I noticed that Orit seemed to like the dish quite a bit, too. As soon as I helped myself to more, she did likewise. Orli then helped herself to some more. Soon, there was only two left on the central plate. The pyramid was no more. Orli gave us one piece each. Pierre did not object. I often noticed Pierre objecting or expressing reservation about consuming the last piece of food. I think it was in keeping with his polite protocol. But his forgetting this protocol was a testimony to how much Pierre liked the dish. Orli was visibly excited that her dish was received so well. I felt, though, that she didn't completely grasp the powerful effect that her dish had on both of us. After that dinner, both Pierre and I bought a half pound of those things every time we went to the Jerusalem Open Market. We tried different vendors and none tasted as good as Orli's. With every taste of other people's grape-leaf-covered-rice-food-piece, we came to appreciate Orli's dish more and more.

This dinner was turning out to be quite a culinary experience. I was glad that we came hungry. Pierre and I did not eat too much that day just in case the food turned out to be not so good. The idea was that since we would be hungry, we would consume whatever was put on our plates, and probably we would look like we were enjoying the food regardless of how good it really was. Now, we found ourselves in the midst of an extraordinary culinary experience. And we were only up to appetizers. Orit said that more was coming, including the main dish. I became more and more glad with each passing second that I starved myself that day. I certainly had room in my stomach for more food, and based on my experience so far, I felt not misguided in expecting a great main dish.

Orit handed out what looked like overgrown pancakes. But the analogy with American pancakes ended with the shape -- circular and flat -- and, perhaps, with composition, which was mostly of flour. The larger pancake before me was as large as a large plate, and in terms of substance it was harder and even somewhat flaky. Orit explained that this dish was a Yemenite dish. One normally consumed this flaky pancake with another ingredient, such as marinated beef or lamb, often wrapped inside the bread pancake. Orit prepared marinated chicken to accompany our Yemenite pancakes. The chicken dish looked sumptuous and smelled quite delicious.

As I looked forward to taking a bite out of the Yemenite pancake and wrapped marinated chicken, I wondered what Pierre was thinking. I knew that there's a pancake in France as well. It's also round and flat like American pancakes, but it's much thinner. Similar to Yemenite pancakes, French pancakes often were consumed with extraneous food matter that was actually essential to the French pancake eating experience. Sometimes, jam or creamy chocolate paste was spread over the French pancakes. I have even heard of some applying pure sugar on the warm French pancakes. Somehow, this was not so appealing for me, but I have tried the chocolate spread. It's quite good.

One fortunate thing about having Pierre as a roommate was that, I came to learn a lot about French culture and such wonderful things as French cuisine. Sometimes, I was introduced to these by Pierre; other times, by beautiful French women who visited Pierre. Pierre had a small group of French friends, and among them were some really nice and talented individuals. One of Pierre's friends actually was quite gifted at making these French pancakes. In fact, she had spent three months in the Alps, one winter, working in a place that specialized in French pancakes. Of course, when Pierre and I learned about this we were enthusiastic. She was kind enough to volunteer to come by one evening and make some of her French pancakes for us.

It wasn't a formal dinner or anything; more like a coffee and desert deal. Pauline was an expert, so each pancake took all of a minute to make. It was quite interesting to see Pauline flip a French pancake in the air when one side was done and she wanted to cook the other side. It looked just as artistic and beautiful as a pizza doe being thrown up in the air by an experienced pizza maker in the streets of New York City. The way Pauline flipped the pancake in the air with minimal and graceful movement of her wrist made the frying pan seem like an extension of her arm. As we consumed the French pancakes, Pauline explained to us that French pancakes can be a dessert in the manner we were consuming them or even a main course meal with meat and vegetable products. They even served them as appetizers. So, it was possible in

Pauline's restaurant in the Alps to have a three course meal made of French pancakes. Pauline also added that the drink of choice for the French pancake meal was apple cider. Pierre agreed and said that next time we'll have to find a good apple cider.

We never had Pauline's French pancakes after that. In fact, somehow, Pierre and I had forgotten about the French pancake with cider event until that night at Orit and Orli's place. This Yemenite pancake experience served as a reminder, and I was resolved to spur Pierre to talk Pauline into coming over and making French pancakes. Pierre and Pauline had such glow on their faces when they talked about eating French pancakes with apple cider, that I wanted to experience that as well. I was wondering if Pierre would bring up French pancakes at that moment in our fellowship dinner with Orit and Orli, but surprisingly he did not.

I was surprised for couple of reasons. Pierre almost never missed an opportunity to extol the merits of French cuisine, especially since it was one of his passions. Also, it would have been a good opportunity for Pierre to transition into a compliment of the Yemenite dish and involve himself in a conversation. Pierre, being the polite Frenchman that he was, almost always had a polite compliment ready particularly when it involved food, and an analogy to French cuisine often accompanied the compliment. Pierre once explained to me that a comparison to French cuisine was a compliment enough since he thought of French cuisine as the best in the world. But, more often than not, Pierre made an explicit reference to individual merits of food in the way of praise. Pierre was careful and polished in that way. I often attributed this to his family background. It might have been that it was just the way Pierre was and not necessarily a product of his social conditioning.

The only conclusion I could deduce at Pierre's lack of ready compliment was that he was nervous. I was almost willing to bet my Yemenite pancake along with the marinated chicken that he was thinking about how he could ask Orli out. Pierre's nervousness was perhaps more accentuated by Orli's outfit. Orli was wearing a sleeveless shirt, which was made from a silky looking substance. And there was a v-shaped collar which revealed that her long neck was just as smooth and unblemished as her beautiful, long tanned arms. Once in a while, I noticed Orli slightly bending forward and even putting her cheeks on her hands as her arms stood vertically on top of the table with her elbows gently pressed against the table cloth. The effect of her movement accentuated the curves of her breast which pressed against the silky shirt. Almost as if helplessly drawn to the beauty of the feminine form, Pierre's eyes were caught lingering in that location by me. This was quite surprising to me because Pierre was usually inconspicuous in his visual appreciation of women. But somehow Pierre's Achilles' heel seemed to have been found.

I felt that I needed to help Pierre, so I particularly concentrated on bringing out Pierre's maximum potential as Pierre. I started complimenting Orit on her dish and gave Pierre a fleeting gaze. Sure enough, Pierre responded and quickly followed suit, almost mechanical, at first. But soon, Pierre was the charming Frenchman that he was, and he started his adulation certainly accompanied by analogies to French cuisine. Pierre even went as far as to say that the Yemenite pancake was better than any French pancakes that he has tasted so far. Knowing Pierre, I was quite impressed by his compliment. Orit and Orli did not know Pierre, then, enough to appreciate the extent of his paean. I felt it my duty to point this out and certainly I did so. I think that the combination of Pierre's compliments and my providing the context for Pierre's compliments had an effect of endearing Pierre further in two ladies' hearts. I noticed Orli looking at Pierre with what I interpreted to be an amorous gaze. Then, I knew that, before the evening was out, Pierre would be going out with Orli or, at least, starting the process in that regard.

While savoring the tasty Yemenite pancakes, I asked Orit about her Yemenite heritage. Orit told me that her grandfather and grandmother came to Israel from Yemen with their families. They were only teenagers, and they traveled on camel back and on foot all the way from Yemen. The story seemed like something out of a novel. I wondered how that must have been like. Orit continued and explained that it wasn't an easy journey, and many people who made such a journey did not make it all the way to Israel. But those who did make it brought a rich culture with them and also some of the most beautiful jewelry in Israel. Orit told me that Yemenite jewelry can be found almost everywhere in Israel. It's quite popular with both young and old. There's even a museum in Jerusalem that houses a collection of original Yemenite Jewelry. When Orit told me this, I quickly turned to Pierre and said that we must visit this museum. Pierre readily agreed. I was looking forward to seeing the Jewelry which was an important part of Orit's history.

Orit was wearing a part of her history on her neck and fingers. She had a beautiful necklace made of silver that adorned her neck. The necklace seemed to suit Orit perfectly. The silver necklace shone under the light against her smooth olive skin. There were some stones imbedded on the necklace, and these colorful stones seemed to carry history in the curious way they shone and reflected light in their place. A stone was at the center of each flat triangular adornment that was attached to the thin silver necklace ring. In fact, the necklace could be summarized as a silver string holding together a chain of silver triangular pieces with embedded stones. But the triangular pieces did not seem like a different part of the necklace in the way a charm hangs down from the necklace. These triangular shaped pieces seemed to be integrated to form a unity in the necklace. The central triangular piece, settled at the bottom of the necklace ring between her two breasts, was the biggest. And the triangular pieces decreased in size along the necklace route heading towards Orit's face, so that the triangular shaped silver pieces were quite small around the sides of her neck below her ears. Orit told me that the necklace was given to her mom by her mom and passed down to her. I thought that it was just simply wonderful that she wore a part of her family history in her person, and I told Orit just that.

Orit was also wearing a couple of rings on her finger. One ring on her right index finger was triangular at the top with the same kind of stone imbedded on the silver ring as the stone imbedded on the central triangular silver piece of her necklace. I found out that this ring was also passed down to her through her mother's side. I thought that this was wonderful and wondered if her other ring was from Yemen, as well. Orit's other ring was in the index finger of her left hand. This was a golden ring with a turquoise colored stone on the top. The stone wasn't a singular color. There were some dark spots on the stone that gave the ring a mythical quality. I asked Orit about this ring, pointing out that it did not seem to fit in with rest of her jewelry. She commented that I was observant and told me that it was a gift for her graduation from her parents. The ring did not have any attachment to Yemen, but rather to Israel. Orit explained that the turquoise stone set on the ring was the Eilat stone.

Eilat is the southernmost city in Israel and is a resort town. It touches the Red Sea, often boasted by many Israelis as the best place to do scubadiving in the world. Some visitors to Israel concur and give the experience two thumbs up. I listened attentively to Orit's explanation. Since I had never scubadived, I had a hard time relating to Orit's enthusiasm over scubadiving merits of Eilat. Orit continued and said that Eilat also has a nice underwater observatory where one can go and see the corals and various exotic fish swimming about under water.

This sounded like something that I would love to explore. I have always been fascinated by the variety and beauty of living creatures. In fact, whenever I travel, I try to visit a zoo or an aquarium. Orit told me that it was also possible to go on a submarine ride, sponsored by the underwater observatory. I thought this would be neat as well. Orit added that all the beauty of the marine life in the Red Sea attracts Israelis and non-Israelis alike to Eilat. Many Israelis have visited Eilat more than a couple of times -- a family vacation, a trip with a group of friends, and even a romantic quest. Eilat provides nice sandy beaches as well, so those who like to lie in the sun and absorb the warmth of the sun can do that, too. Orit explained that the sand was actually transported to the area because Eilat's beaches naturally tend to be rocky. This was a good move by Israel's tourist industry since rocky beaches do not make for a good tourist spot. Eilat is constantly expanding and adding new hotels to accommodate the ever growing number of tourists from all over the world.

Orit gave a personal account of her experience in Eilat. Orit has been down to Eilat at least seven times herself. In fact, Orit liked Eilat and the Red Sea so much that her parents started to call her, Bat Yam, or The Daughter of the Sea. This nickname stuck with her and even her friends refer to her as Bat Yam. Orit told me that she feels free when she explores the marine life of the Red Sea. The sea seems boundless and as much as she swims in it there doesn't seem to be an end, Orit ex-plained. Orit added that when she's in the Red Sea, she feels like one of the happy fish that she sometimes chases under water for fun.

Once, she commented, one of the fish that she was chasing turned around and started to chase her. She said that it was an exhilarating experience to play a tag game with a fish. Orit said that she felt like she was accepted into the fish world. She was one of them swimming to and fro. And the fish in the Red Sea are so colorful. Being near them, seeing them up close, even touching them are experiences that one will not forget. The variety of the fish population in the Red Sea is so amazing, Orit added, that she sometimes played this game with her friends, human friends, of trying to find a resemblance be-tween a swimming fish and someone they knew. Fish in the Red Sea are of all shapes, sizes, and distinctive qualities, so it wasn't too hard to find a fish that has a quality that stand out that reminds one of a familiar person.

Orit continued her praise of Eilat and explained that she enjoyed walking along the sandy beach particularly as the sun was setting because she was able to see the coastlines of Jordan, Egypt, and even Saudi Arabia. Orit proclaimed that the glowing, beautiful sun-shine along the colorful horizon promised harmony and future peace in the region. The way that the waters sometimes reflected the descending sun rays and even glittered brightly even to the point of blinding one's eyes seemed like a certain promise of hope. A stamp of promise from above. As heaven and earth seemed to be united in the descending sun, the waters of the Red Sea seemed to be the best testimony to this harmony. Orit's beauti-ful eyes reflected what she saw in the Red Sea by the descending sun light as they captured the light in the room and glittered brightly.

I was convinced. Next time that there was a long weekend opportunity, I was going to head down to Eilat. After all, it's not so far away from Jerusalem. Orit said something like four to five hours on the bus, which goes directly from Jerusalem to Eilat. I wondered if it would be possible to go to Eilat with Orit. I knew that I would have abundance of treasure in memories, if that could be possible.

Then, Orli interjected that it was time for dessert. I was quite satiated from the meal. I wasn't sure if I could eat anymore. The meal was filling and fulfilling in terms of all my expectations and more. But when I saw that it was a chocolate cake, I knew that I could make room for more food. It looked beautiful. It was rectangular in shape, and there was a smooth chocolate frosting on the top. And it smelled wonderful. Orli explained that they just made the cake that day. It was quite touching that Orit and Orli made such a great effort for this dinner. Before I had a chance to express my thanks, Pierre jumped in and expressed his pleasure at seeing the chocolate cake and thanks for the effort that they put in. Pierre was looking at Orli most of the time while he was dispensing his complements. And they were quite profuse but with a flare of gracefulness that was so characteristic of Pierre. I thought to myself that this was good, especially since I was rooting for Pierre to get together with Orli.

Orli seemed to like the complement and sent one of her sweet smiles to Pierre. Pierre answered Orli's missive with the brightest smile that I have seen on his face to date. And the cake was very good. I was more impressed to find out that it was the first time that Orli and Orit made the cake. They made it for us, since they knew that we liked chocolate and thought that chocolate cake was a characteristic dessert both in France and America. I thought that this was really thoughtful. I felt myself blessed that I had the opportunity to get to know Orit and Orli. Who would have thought that a chance meeting at a bus stop would turn into something beautiful like this?

I am deeply emerged in my thoughts and remembrance, looking out the window into the clear skies of Bat Yam and endless water that blended into the sky in the distant horizon. I cannot help but smile. And in the corner of my eye, I catch my own reflection in the window. I notice how much darker my skin has become. The Mediterranean sun has been a warm source of nourishment for my skin, and I am not displeased by the golden brown, healthy skin hue that I see before me on the window. Swimming in the waters of Bat Yam certainly contributed to the present golden brown state of my skin tone.

Before I have a chance to submerge myself further in thought and remembrance of all the happy memories of Bat Yam, the phone rings. I quickly rush over to the phone, knowing that it is Pierre. I pick up the receiver and surely it is Pierre on the line. Pierre begins by apologizing for the delay. Some things happened that held him up. Pierre assures me that they are good things and tells me not to worry. He will explain everything when he gets back to the apartment. Pierre then asks, if Orit has arrived, yet. I look at the time and notice that Orit is five minutes late. I tell Pierre that she hasn't, yet. Pierre says that he will be back in five to ten minutes and hangs up the phone. Just then, the door bell rings. I open the door and there is Orit, Bat Yam, the Daughter of the Sea, in all her glory.

About the Author

H. C. Kim has lived over three years in Israel with fellowships from the Israeli government and various Jewish agencies. H. C. Kim is an expert on Jewish studies and has taught the subject at UCLA and Brown University. He is fluent in modern Hebrew and particularly appreciates ancient Hebrew poetry, especially from the Second Temple period. The Hebrew University of Jerusalem in Israel profiled him in a two page article in their alumni magazine, and H. C. Kim was featured as a key star in the promotional video for the university that was distributed to Jewish agencies around the world.

www.ingramcontent.com/pod-product-compliance
Lightning Source LLC
Chambersburg PA
CBHW030130180626
46812CB00002B/634